D0496946

Creatures

If You Go Down to the Woods

"It's gone!" Caroly whispered. Her face was dead white and she looked as if she was going to be sick. "But how? It can't have *walked*!"

"Can't it?" said Alex. The horrible thought she had had earlier was creeping back. The owl. The fox. The bag. All those tracks in the snow.

And Chaz. . .

"They're coming alive," she said in a small, fearful voice. "The animals in our props and costume bits . . . They're *all* coming alive!"

Look for other Creatures titles
by Louise Cooper:

1 Once I Caught a Fish Alive
3 See How They Run

Creatures

If You Go Down to the Woods

Louise Cooper

For Jamie and Will Randall; with thanks – I think! – for reminding me just how long it is since I was at school!

Scholastic Children's Books
Commonwealth House, 1–19 New Oxford Street,
London WC1A 1NU, UK
London ~ New York ~ Toronto ~ Sydney ~ Auckland
Mexico City ~ New Delhi ~ Hong Kong
First published by Scholastic Ltd, 1998

ISBN 0 590 11163 9

Typeset by Falcon Oast Graphic Art
Printed by Cox & Wyman Ltd., Reading, Berks

10 9 8 7 6 5 4 3

1

"I must be mad!"

Alexandra Birnie – Alex to her friends – stopped in the middle of the busy High Street as she said the words aloud. People looked at her; a few sniggered, as if they agreed, but she took no notice. She just stared at the bag in her hand. A hat, long gloves and a fox-fur wrap. She *was* mad.

But then, the junk shop in the scruffy little side road had been just about her last hope. As wardrobe mistress for the school's Christmas panto, she had been getting desperate. Only two weeks to go before the show opened, and Horrida, the Wicked Stepmother, hadn't got a costume. Alex knew the kind of thing she wanted – a kind of 1920s Cruella de Vil look. But finding it hadn't been so easy. Until she had gone into that grotty old shop, and there they were.

The fox fur was staring at her from a shelf, and it gave her quite a fright when she first saw it. The hat was next to it; it had a huge brim and was literally covered in feathers of every kind imaginable. And beside the hat were the gloves, made of what looked horribly like snake skin and trimmed with three different types of fur.

Alex felt a rush of mixed pity and fury for all the dead animals. The thought that they had been killed just to decorate human beings disgusted her. But then she remembered the panto. Awful though they were, these would be perfect for Horrida; and besides, they must be at least fifty years old. Not that that changed the principle, but . . . well, the poor things had died such a long time ago that it couldn't make any difference to them now.

The woman behind the counter said, "Three quid the lot. Take 'em or leave 'em, but stop messing 'em around. I don't like kids who mess things around."

Alex wanted to retort that *she* didn't like grumpy people who smelled of mothballs. Instead she heard herself saying, "I'll take them." And suddenly here she was, counting out three pound coins and watching as Grumpy shoved the objects into a scrumpled carrier-bag.

What on earth made me do that? she asked herself. *These are horrible! A dead fox, and the skins and feathers of heaven alone knows how many other creatures . . . I'll have nightmares!*

But it was too late to change her mind. Grumpy wasn't the sort to give her her money back. It looked as if Wicked Stepmother Horrida was going to have her costume after all.

Alex peered cautiously into the carrier-bag. The fox's head with its glass eyes stared back at her. It, too, smelled of mothballs – and of something else that she couldn't place. Foxes, probably. She continued to stare at it, until a jingling sound nearby startled her back to earth.

She looked up, and saw a mournful-looking man standing a few paces away, rattling a collecting box. He must have moved up very quietly – Alex was sure he hadn't been there a minute ago – and with a flush of guilt she realized that he was collecting for a wildlife charity. Turning hot and cold together, she closed the bag quickly, then fumbled for her purse. She couldn't walk past and ignore him, not carrying this. She didn't have the nerve.

She grabbed the first coin she could find and put it into the box without even checking to see what it was. Only as it dropped from her fingers and vanished through the slot did she realize that she'd given away a pound. Almost her last one, as well. *Serves me right,* she thought.

The man had also seen what the coin was, and his mournful look vanished. He beamed and thanked her, and Alex's face turned scarlet with shame. Before he could give her a sticker (which, to her dismay, had a fox's head on it), she hurried off, ducking past him and almost running towards the bus stop.

Panto rehearsals were held on weekdays after lessons, but weekends were devoted to what Mr Lawless, the art teacher, called "the back-room stuff". So every Saturday the school hall was given over to scene-painting, costume-creating and all the other nuts and bolts of the production.

By the time Alex arrived, work was in full

swing. The hall stage was a glorious muddle of wood, cardboard, trestle tables and paint pots, and Mr Lawless (who was also directing the show and playing Baron Beastly) was slapping violent green emulsion on to a huge cardboard flat.

"Hello, Alex!" he greeted her. "You're late!"

"Sorry, Mr Lawless. I was in town and had to wait ages for a bus." Alex brandished her carrier. "But I've found a costume for Horrida."

"Have you, now?" Mr Lawless came over, wiping paint off his glasses. He was the nicest of all the teachers, very tall and lanky and with unfashionably long hair and a dry sense of humour. He was also an extremely good artist – though looking at the half-painted flat, that was hard to believe at the moment.

"Is it going to be that colour when it's finished?" Alex asked dubiously.

"What? Oh, the green – gruesome, isn't it?" Mr Lawless said cheerfully. "Don't worry; it won't look like that under stage lights. That's one of the secrets of scene-painting. Now –" extending a green-splodged hand – "let's see what you've got for Horrida."

Alex's sister Caroly, who was also a back-stage helper, had seen her arrive and came hurrying across. "What's in there?" She peered into the bag that Mr Lawless had opened and her eyes widened. "Oh, *yuk*!"

Mr Lawless fished out the fox-fur wrap and held it up. "Well, whatever it is," he said, "it's certainly very dead, which is one small mercy."

"It's *horrible*!" said Caroly furiously. "A *fox* – oh my God! And feathers, and more fur, and those gloves – Alex, how *could* you?"

Caroly was three years younger than Alex, and fancied herself as one of the school's leading eco-warriors. She started to say all the things that Alex had already said to herself, but before it could turn into an argument Mr Lawless intervened.

"Hold on, Caroly. That's the whole point, isn't it? The Wicked Stepmother's an evil character, so we want the audience to hate her." He grinned. "Which they certainly will if she wears this lot. We'll have every animal rights activist in town yelling for her blood."

"Dead right!" Caroly said indignantly. "Alex, you're *disgusting!*"

"Hey, give her a break," said Mr Lawless. "She didn't kill the poor things herself!" He put the fox back, then sniffed the bag. "By the look and smell of it, they'd all have died naturally a very long time ago, anyway."

"That's not the point—" Caroly persisted.

"OK, OK, but what I mean is, there's nothing any of us can do to put things right after all this time, is there? So we might as well use them. In fact," Mr Lawless added, "we could put a few extra lines in the script, about cruelty to wildlife."

Caroly scowled. "That's not enough! We shouldn't *even touch* those things – it's sickening, and Alex shouldn't have done it!"

"All right, Caroly, we've got the message!" Mr Lawless said. "So now we'll put it across in the script. But not *too* heavily – this is supposed to be a comedy, remember?" He gestured towards the stage. "And now that's settled, how about you two getting down to some hard work?"

It was a terrifying thought that in just two weeks *So What and the Seven Dwarfs* must be ready for the opening night. It certainly terrified Alex whenever she thought about it, especially as she had three different jobs. As well as being wardrobe mistress, she was also understudying a dwarf called Dippy (very appropriate, everyone said) and was second in charge, after Mr Lawless, of the scenery painting.

At least Horrida's costume was sorted out now. Mags Freeman, who was playing the wicked stepmother, shrieked with laughter when she saw what Alex had found for her.

"They're brilliant – really gross!" she said gleefully. Pulling the fox fur from the bag she draped it round her neck and struck a Horrida-like pose. "The audience is going to absolutely *hate* me!"

Caroly shuddered, but Alex felt enormous relief. Caroly had had another go at her about the dead animals, and several others had put their oars in, too. But it was Mags who mattered, and when it came to squeamish feelings Mags was about as sensitive as a concrete post. She was trying the hat on now, tilting it at a rakish angle on her mass of frizzy blonde hair. Then she pulled an awful face and announced theatrically,

"Mirror, mirror, on the wall, who is the fairest of them all?"

The fact that Mags was bigger than most of the boys in the school and, to put it politely, plump, meant that line was guaranteed to bring the house down. Alex grinned. "They'll hate you *and* love you," she said cheerfully. "Better take them off now, though. We've still got the dress to finish."

"OK." Reluctantly Mags dumped the hat on the table, then started to unwind the fur. "I'll just – ow!" She jumped, and sucked at her thumb.

"What's the matter?" Alex asked.

"Something stuck in me. Must be a pin hidden in here." Gingerly Mags ran her hand over the fox's head. "Can't find anything. But it really hurt. Hey, it's bleeding – look."

Alex saw the bright scarlet bead on Mags's thumb, and frowned. "That's weird," she said. "It doesn't look like a pin-prick. It's more like. . ." Her voice tailed off.

"More like what?" Mags prompted.

But suddenly Alex didn't want to say what she thought it looked like. Because the whole notion was utterly ridiculous and couldn't possibly be right.

Aloud, she replied, "Oh . . . I don't know. A cut or something. Leave it on the table, Mags, and I'll have a good look later and find out what it was."

Mags forgot the incident almost immediately. In the bustle of work Alex soon forgot it, too. Though now and again she did recall it briefly, and when she did she felt a twinge of puzzlement.

Small though it was, the mark on Mags's thumb had looked as if it had been made by *teeth*.

2

By the time she got home that evening, all Alex wanted to do was flop in front of the TV for a couple of hours and then go to bed.

The only consolation was that they had achieved a lot today. The scenery for the wood was almost finished, and Mr Lawless had rigged up a couple of lights to show how it would look on stage. Alex had made five dwarfs' hats, and So What (alias Devi Gupta, who was sickeningly beautiful with hair nearly down to her knees) had looked hilarious in her finished grunge costume.

On the bus home, sharing the seat with piles of bags and parcels, Alex yawned as she tried to remember all the things she had to do. Horrida's dress to finish, then two dwarfs' outfits, a new tail for the pantomime horse, and a bobble hat and football scarf for Baron Beastly. Oh, and the Fairy Godfather still didn't have a machine-gun. What on earth could she find that could be made to look like a machine-gun? There was a limit to what you could do with empty loo rolls and Sellotape. . .

She yawned again. She needed a bath; however hard she tried, it seemed impossible not to get covered in paint at these sessions. Her stop was coming up; she got to her feet and counted her bags. There should have been six, but there were only five. Where the heck had the other one got to?

Alex fished under her seat, but the sixth bag wasn't there. Muttering, she started to rummage in earnest. The bus was slowing down. If she wasn't quick she'd miss her stop.

Suddenly she saw the missing carrier. It had fetched up two seats away, wedged against the hump where the bus wheel was. Alex couldn't imagine how it had got there but she was too relieved to worry. She snatched it up, apologizing to a pair of feet that got in her way. It was the bag with the fox fur in it, too; she would really have been in trouble if she'd lost that.

The bus rumbled to a halt, and Alex jumped down to the pavement and headed for home.

A bath, a meal and a video later, Alex fell thankfully into bed. The costume bags were dumped on her bedroom floor; she'd clear them up tomorrow, but for now she was too tired to care.

She was asleep within five minutes, and slept soundly. Until something broke into her dreams.

Alex snapped awake so suddenly that her heart thumped. The room was dark except for a faint glow from the street lamp outside, and when she looked at her clock she saw that it was just after two a.m.

She frowned up at the ceiling, wondering what had disturbed her. Then, as her mind grew less fuzzy, she became aware of the noise.

At first it seemed to come from somewhere outside, and it sounded very much like rain. But after a minute or so Alex decided that there was something odd about it. Rain swooshed and pattered. This was more of a rustling, dry rather than wet. In fact it wasn't quite like anything she could remember ever hearing before.

She sat up, curious. As she did so, she realized something else. The sound wasn't coming from outside. It was much closer.

It was in the room with her.

Alex's heart lurched a second time, and her skin started to prickle and crawl. She wanted to turn her head and look around, but she was suddenly too frightened to move. The soft rustling continued. It was a very *steady* sound. And it was getting closer, as if something was moving slowly but relentlessly across the floor towards her.

Her pulse was pounding like hammers now, and desperately she swivelled her gaze, trying to see into the room's corners. The street lamp showed the dim outlines of furniture, and Alex knew she could easily lose control and believe that those outlines were moving. They weren't, of course. They couldn't be. They weren't alive.

But something in here was. . .

She shut her eyes and forced herself to take a deep breath. This was stupid. Her imagination was running riot and she had to calm down. Just one second, that was all it would take to reach out to the lamp on the table beside her. *For God's sake,* she thought, *it's only a few centimetres away! Do it – just do it!*

With her eyes still tightly shut, her hand shot out. Her fingers touched the lampshade and she almost knocked the whole thing over. A frantic grab saved it and she scrabbled for the switch, fumbling and gasping with the terror of suspense. She felt as if the darkness beyond her eyelids was about to pounce, and a voice inside her screamed in silent fear: *The rustling's getting louder, it's getting louder—*

With a click the lamp came on – and instantly the rustling stopped.

Slowly, Alex opened her eyes. The lamplight seemed glaringly bright and harsh, making her blink as she stared nervously at the room. It was very quiet, and everything looked absolutely normal. There was her desk and chair. Her bookshelf. Her cassette radio. The wardrobe door was closed, as she had left it. Even the bags of panto costumes still lay on the floor where she had dropped them. Alex glanced at the bags, and—

"*Aah!*" It came out as a squeak rather than a scream, which was just as well, as her parents were asleep in the next room. Alex put a hand to her mouth, pushing down half-hysterical laughter and calling herself a prize idiot. It wasn't a small and horrible monster that was glaring up at her from among the bags – it was only the fox-fur wrap! The junk shop carrier had fallen over, tipping some of its contents on to the carpet, and the fur was among them. It was partly hidden behind the other bags, so that only the head showed, and for a moment it had looked so real that it frightened the life out of Alex.

Her laughter dissolved into a snort. The supposedly "eerie" rustling must have been made by the plastic bag slowly uncrumpling itself after it fell over. That was a *really* dumb thing to be scared of!

All the same, though, the fox's head was a bit creepy. She didn't fancy the idea of those glass eyes staring at her all night, so she got out of bed and went to pick the fur up. She'd just shove it back in the bag, out of sight, then maybe she could get some sleep.

The fox fur felt very warm to her touch, and it seemed to smell mustier than before. *Better open the window in the morning*, Alex thought, *or Mum will hit the roof*.

She bundled the fur away. Some feathers from the hat had also come off and spilled from the bag; she gathered them up, wondering how on earth they could have managed to spread themselves so far across the floor. That would mean a tricky glueing job tomorrow. Boring.

Alex climbed back into bed. She took a last look round the room, just to be certain that everything was as it should be. No creeping shadows. No strange noises. *Idiot*. The rustling bag had set her off, and she'd imagined the whole thing.

With the fear gone and her pulse back to normal, she switched the lamp off and settled down.

When the rustling began again, it was very quiet, almost furtive. As if something had learned a small lesson, and was taking the greatest care not to wake her a second time. . .

3

Sunday didn't start well for Alex. First there was Mum, who came into her bedroom at half-past eight demanding to know what "that horrible smell" was. Struggling out of sleep – she *had* wanted a lie-in – Alex started to say, "What sm—?" then stopped as it hit her nostrils.

"Urgh!" She sat up in bed, pulling a face. "Where's *that* coming from?"

"You tell me!" said Mum. "The stink reaches half way down the landing! It smells like an old dog that hasn't been bathed for years!"

Alex looked round, then saw the carrier-bags. "Oh. . ." she said.

The fox fur was the culprit all right. Alex couldn't imagine why she hadn't noticed it before; it was probably the central heating bringing the pong out.

"You're doing more scene-painting at school this afternoon, aren't you?" Mum said. "Right, then you can leave the bag in the garden until you go. And if you expect poor Mags to wear it on stage, you'd better get it fumigated first!"

Even when Mum used a whole can of Daffodil Dell room spray, the smell didn't disappear completely. Then Alex had to listen to another self-righteous lecture from Caroly about animal rights. There was no point Alex reminding her that she'd heard it all before, and she was only thankful that their older sister, Tess, was away at college and couldn't put her oar in, too.

Alex spent most of the morning struggling with Horrida's dress and Mum's ancient sewing machine. Lunch was roast chicken, which started Caroly off again. Alex ignored the mutterings about battery farming and how the whole world ought to be vegetarian, but when Caroly used the chicken as another excuse to snipe at her about the fox fur, she had had enough.

"And what do you think foxes eat?" she demanded stroppily. "Tofu burgers and brown rice? No, they don't; they eat chickens, just like us. *And* they're not nice about the way they kill them! They tear them to bits and—"

"Oh, shut up! It's totally different!"

"No, it isn't, and if you had the brains to think, instead of just repeating what all your dumb so-called friends tell you—"

"What do you know about thinking?" Caroly snarled. "You're a murderer! An animal murderer!"

Dad intervened then and told them to stop squabbling or he wouldn't give either of them a lift that afternoon and they could both walk. Silence fell at the table. Alex and Caroly glowered at each other. Then, very slowly and deliberately, Alex speared a huge forkful of chicken, put it in her mouth and mumbled with relish, "Mmmm . . . *lovely*!"

Two spots of furious colour flamed on Caroly's cheeks and her eyes became venomous. "You wait," she said under her breath. "Just you *wait*. . ."

"That's enough, Caroly!" Mum warned. "Alex, you ought to know better than to wind her up. You're old enough to be sensible. And don't talk with your mouth full. It's rude."

After lunch Dad gave both the girls the

promised lift, Alex to the school and Caroly (who wasn't helping today) to a friend's house. The smell from the fox fur was still noticeable; Dad drove with the windows wide open, and at the school gates Caroly said snidely, "Going to go and strangle the school's gerbils, then?" Alex was glad to escape.

An extra helper was in the hall when Alex arrived. It was Mr Lawless's wife, Imogen. Imogen (she said they must all call her by her first name) was a sculptress, and as offbeat as her husband. Though she was probably older than Alex's and her friends' parents, she wore long, floaty skirts in bright colours and her blonde hair hung down to her waist, with tiny plaits woven into it. She greeted Alex with a grin and a wave, but before Alex could wave back, Mags pounced energetically on her.

"Hey, Alex, come and look at this! My nan dug it out of her junk cupboard; it was her grandad's, and she says we can have it for the panto!"

"It" was standing on a trestle table at the back of the stage. It was a stuffed owl, sitting on a branch on a wooden pedestal.

Alex stared in amazement, and Mags said gleefully, "Gross, isn't it?" "Gross" was Mags's favourite word. "We'll put it on a table next to the mirror, and I can do a sort of double-act with it. If Mr Lawless fixes up some sound effects for it, then—"

"Hey, wait a minute!" called Mr Lawless, who had overheard. "Brilliant artist, virtuoso actor, and now you expect me to be a sound engineer, too?" He came over. "Mind you, the basic notion's good. Maybe we can get someone to stand behind the scenery and make the noises."

"What sort of noises?" Mags was getting into the idea.

"Oh, I don't know . . . squawks or squeaks or whatever owls do. No, hang on; owls hoot, don't they?"

"*Whoo-hoo-hoooo!*" Mags mimicked sepulchrally, and shrieked with laughter. "*Too-wit, too-whoo-hoo! Ooooh – So What is fairer than yoo-hoo-hoooo! So, pooooh!*"

"Great! The owl talks like that, and we'll make it rhyme along with the rest of the script. Robbie Blake's doing the voice of the mirror, so he can have a go at the owl, too. Now," Mr Lawless grinned at them both. "Imogen and I have got some things to contribute, too. We thought we'd wait until Alex arrived before we showed them to you. What do you think of these?"

From a black plastic bin-bag he produced a stag's head, complete with antlers, mounted on a plaque. As the girls goggled at it, he fished in the bag again.

"And this is for Horrida." Out came a large, old-fashioned handbag, with a concertina-type opening at the top and a large clasp. The outside was scaly.

"One crocodile-skin bag," said Imogen. "Not the real thing, of course; it's a complete fake. It belonged to my Great-Auntie Hydrangea or someone, and I've been looking for an excuse to get rid of it for years."

"It looks pretty convincing," said Alex, rubbing a hand over it. "What *is* it made of?"

"Oh, I don't know. Plastic or something – if they'd invented plastic in those days, that is. There you are, Mags, try it for size."

Mags hung the bag on her arm and strutted across the stage. "Great!" she said. "It really swings well. Hey, you know that scene where I have to hit Baron Beastly—"

"Remember who's playing Baron Beastly, thank you!" said Mr Lawless. "That thing could pack quite a punch!"

Mags grinned. "I promise I'll be careful, Mr L."

Alex was still gazing at the stag. Caroly would go ballistic when she saw it, she thought, and it would be no good talking about the damage deer could do to crops and woodlands. Still, at least the handbag wasn't real. That was something.

Mags suggested that maybe the stag's head could talk, too, and started to try out some voices for it. Alex looked uneasily around for Caroly. Remembering she'd gone to a friend's house, she breathed a sigh of relief.

"Come on, Mags," she said. "Try your dress on and let's see how everything looks together."

"*Oka-hay-hay!*" Mags sounded like a whinnying horse, and her nose wrinkled. "Nah – that's no good for a stag's voice, is it?"

"Lousy," said Alex. "If I were you, I'd—"

She stopped, staring at the owl on its perch.

"What's up?" Mags asked.

"N-nothing. . ." But there was. Because the owl had *blinked*.

"Alex?" Mr Lawless looked at her face and frowned.

Alex shook her head. "It isn't anything. Honestly. I'm . . . fine."

"You don't look it. You've gone white. Do you want a drink of water?"

"No, really, thanks. I'm OK now; I just thought. . ."

They waited, but she couldn't explain, even to herself. The owl wasn't alive. It was dead. Stuffed. A dead, stuffed owl could not *possibly* blink. No way. No way at all.

Your brain's not in gear, Alex, she told herself. *Wake up, all right? Just wake up, and stop imagining things!*

She looked at the owl again. The owl stared back with blank, empty eyes. It was completely motionless.

"Right, Mags," said Alex with determined cheerfulness, "let's get you into the dress!"

By the end of the day, they had achieved quite a lot. Mags's dress fitted, to Alex's huge relief, and with the fur, the gloves, the hat and the handbag she was really starting to look how everyone imagined Horrida. They finished the woodland scenery and made a start on the inside of the castle, and Chaz Peterson, who was the Fairy Godfather, turned up with a garish yellow-and-green plastic Startrooper Laser Exterminator. It had been his kid brother's until he got bored with it, and with a bit of disguising it would make a great machine gun.

And, best of all, Caroly wasn't there.

Alex was very thankful to have avoided yet another harangue about animal welfare. All the same, as she was packing up at the end of the day, she had to admit to herself that Caroly had a point. There was something very sad about the growing pile of animal bits and pieces in the props box. There were so *many* animals involved. Foxes, rabbits, deer, birds . . . the list seemed to be getting longer and longer. It was depressing to think that human beings could be that cruel. And the sight of the fur and the feathers and the dead, glassy-eyed faces all together in the box was more than a little bit creepy.

A voice calling from the hall doors startled her out of her thoughts. "All right, Alex? Come on, I've got to lock up."

Mr Lawless was waiting, with his hand on the light switch. Shutting the box, Alex grabbed her coat, jumped down from the stage and ran to join him.

"Got everything?" he asked. "Right, here we go, then."

He turned the lights off and the hall was plunged into gloom. Alex looked back at the stage. She could just make out the painted flats left propped against the wall. The woodland scenes looked weirdly convincing. . .

Then, as Mr Lawless started to pull the door shut, she heard a noise.

"What was that?"

"What was what?" Mr Lawless asked.

"I thought I heard something. . ."

"In the hall?" He peered. "Oh, blast! I think those trestle tables I propped up have fallen over again. Never mind, I'll sort them out in the morning. Can't stop now, Imogen and I are going out for an extremely hot curry." He paused. "Are you OK for getting home?"

"Yes, thanks," said Alex. "Mags's mum's giving me a lift."

At the main door she waved goodbye to Mr Lawless and started towards the gates, where Mags's mother would be waiting. The outside security light was still on, but the path was dark and everything seemed unusually quiet. Hurrying, Alex suddenly heard what sounded like pattering footsteps behind her. She looked round.

The pattering stopped. There was no one else there. But she was just in time to glimpse a shadow skittering into one of the bushes beside the path. The bush shook, rustled. Then there was only stillness.

"Hello. . .?" Alex called cautiously. Her heart was starting to beat uncomfortably fast. "Who's that?"

No answer. The security light still glared. In the distance, she heard Mr and Mrs Lawless's car start up.

And she could *smell* something. Something strong, almost rank.

An *animal* smell. . .

For no sensible reason whatever, Alex suddenly remembered the peculiar noise in her bedroom last night. It was stupid, because she knew what had caused that: just a carrier-bag rustling.

Except that the rustle in the bush had sounded unnervingly similar. . .

Alex backed away a pace, then another. She couldn't shake off an awful feeling that someone or something was *watching* her. And that same someone – or something – was *angry*.

She swallowed, very hard, and called out quaveringly again: "Hello. . .?"

"Hiya!" The answer came so unexpectedly that she almost physically jumped on the spot. A shadow loomed against the light, and Chaz Peterson appeared.

"Hi, Alex. You lost something?" Chaz, skinny

and gangly, looked down at her and grinned. "Or are you just daydreaming again?"

Am I? Alex asked herself. She knew that her vagueness was a bit of a joke in her year. This time, though, she hadn't been daydreaming, as Chaz put it. Not at all.

With an effort she pulled her mind together, and said nonchalantly, "I was just waiting for you, Chaz. In case you were scared of the dark."

"Ha, ha." Chaz pulled a face at her. "Want to walk home with me?"

Alex's heart was thumping like a sledgehammer now. "No." *Definitely not*, she thought. *I just want to get out of here, and fast.* "I'm getting a lift. See you."

Chaz shrugged and walked away. Alex made herself stand still until he was out of sight. Then, without looking back at the school building, she sprinted for the gate.

4

Alex didn't get another lecture from Caroly. Caroly spent the whole evening in her room. She didn't even come downstairs to watch her favourite wildlife TV programme, and when she did finally appear, and Mum asked her what she had been doing, she was very secretive. Alex was relieved.

Until, at lunchtime the next day, she found out what her sister had been up to.

Eight of Caroly's Year Seven friends were waiting for her as she came out of the school canteen. Caroly was at the head of the group, and she stepped into Alex's path.

"This," Caroly said in a loud, self-important

voice, "is for *you*."

The others all glared as Alex took the piece of paper that Caroly held out. It had been done on a computer, and it was headlined "ANIMAL MURDERERS", with garish red graphics that made the page look as if it was splattered with blood.

Alex started to read the wording.

"We, the undersinged" – pity Caroly couldn't learn to spell, she thought – "DEMAND an end to the ANIMAL CRUELTY in the school pantamime. All stage props using ANIMAL skins, fur, feathers and etc. are EXPLOTATIVE and UNACEPTABLE and we DEMAND that you do not use them. We also DEMAND that you give £5 to an ANIMAL charity to be chosen by us in COMPENSATION."

Underneath were about thirty signatures.

Alex looked at Caroly. Caroly stared aggressively back. "Well?" she said.

"That's a lot of demands, from a bunch of kids," Alex retorted.

"Well, you'd better take notice of them!"

The others muttered and nodded. Alex swept them all with a filthy look. "And what if I don't?"

"You'll regret it," Caroly told her savagely. "That's a promise!"

Alex would have liked nothing better at that moment than to give her sister a good kicking. She squashed the feeling, and instead gave the petition a last, sneering look before pushing it back under Caroly's nose.

"When I want advice about the panto, I'll ask someone with a brain," she said scornfully. "Shove off, and take this garbage with you. I'm not impressed!"

Caroly shouted something after her as she stalked away, but Alex neither knew nor cared what it was. A petition, indeed! As if she was personally responsible for the deaths of all those animals! Then suddenly her anger melted and she grinned to herself. How about skinning all those Year Sevens and using them instead? That would do the world a favour. The grin became a giggle as she had a brief, delicious vision of Mr Lawless's plaque with Caroly's head on it in place of the stag's. She could stick the antlers on with Sellotape. . .

"What's so funny, then?" said a voice behind her, and Alex turned to see Mags catching her up.

"Oh . . . nothing, really." Alex grinned again. "You haven't got a sister, have you?"

"No, thanks!"

"Well, watch out for mine. And the rest of the eco-warriors."

"Oh, right. Going to sabotage us or something, are they?"

"Or something."

"I wouldn't worry if I were you," said Mags. "Any trouble, and I'll just belt them with my mock-croc handbag." Her eyes sparked wickedly. "Knock 'em out for a week. That thing's *heavy*." Then she paused, peering more closely at Alex's face. "You're not *really* worried, are you?"

"Course not."

But deep down, Alex wasn't so sure.

On Tuesday morning, Alex opened her locker and found *MURDERER* written in black marker pen on the inside of the door.

It didn't take a genius to know who had done it; she even recognized the writing. Caroly.

"That little—" Alex bit back what she wanted to call her sister, and told herself to be reasonable. It was only a word. Caroly was a kid, and kids got over-enthusiastic. She hadn't actually *done* anything.

Yet, said an inner voice. Alex ignored it. She wouldn't give Caroly the satisfaction of letting this get to her. She'd just stick a poster over the graffiti and forget about it.

She shoved her coat into the locker, slammed the door, and walked off to her first class.

There was a panto rehearsal after school, and today they were going to try some of the scenes with props and costumes for the first time. Caroly wasn't there, to Alex's relief, and she and Mr Lawless started dragging the scenery into place, trying to avoid the gaggle of younger kids who had a dance to do in the big woodland scene. The music teacher, Miss Macey (known behind her back as Mousey or, more often, Squeak), was standing by the piano and yelling uselessly at the dancers to "be *quiet*!", while behind the curtains So What and Horrida were doing each other's hair, and the Fairy Godfather, complete with pin-striped suit and Al Capone hat, swung the "machine-gun" around and made loud, stuttering noises.

"Chaz, will you shut *up*!" Mr Lawless barged him out of the way as he and Alex lugged the biggest flat into place. "If you can't find anything better to do, go and get some props. We want the mirror for Horrida's boudoir. And get the stag's head; we'll experiment with a behind-the-scenes voice for it. Go *on*!"

"OK." Chaz made a last sweep with the machine-gun, winked at Alex (who stuck her tongue out in return) and sauntered off.

With a bit more grunting and heaving the flat was positioned, and as Alex stepped back, Mags emerged from behind the curtain.

"Look at me!" she said. "Hey-hey – what do you think?"

She had the full costume on – dress, hat, gloves, and a pair of scarlet stiletto-heeled shoes, with the fox fur draped dramatically over her shoulders.

"Wow!" Alex grinned. "That's great, Mags! You look really evil!"

At that moment Chaz came back, empty-handed.

"Mr Lawless," he said, "you said there was a stag's head."

"That's right. It's in the props box with everything else."

Chaz shook his head. "It isn't. But I found this."

"This" was a piece of paper. Mr Lawless took it, and the others peered round him to read it.

It had been done on a computer, like the petition, and it said, in large red capital letters:

"THE DEER HAS BEEN GIVEN

SANCTURY. THIS IS JUST THE START."

"I don't believe it," Mr Lawless said disgustedly. He looked suddenly, suspiciously, at Alex. "Has your sister got anything to do with this?"

"I'll bet anything she has!" Alex growled through clenched teeth. "This is just her style."

"And of course she isn't here, is she? No, I thought not." Mr Lawless sighed exasperatedly. "Well, there's not much we can do about it now. We'd better get on with the rehearsal. But you can tell Caroly from me that if that head isn't brought back, she's in big trouble!"

"Don't you worry, Mr Lawless," said Alex grimly. "I'll tell her a lot more than that!"

As Mr Lawless stomped off, Mags drew Alex aside and whispered, "What's she *done* with it? Someone must have seen her – I mean, a stag's head isn't the sort of thing you can just shove in your pocket and walk off with, is it?"

"Right." Caroly's locker was the first obvious place, Alex thought. Failing that, the head was probably somewhere in the school grounds. But she wasn't going to waste time searching for it. There were much quicker ways.

"I'll get her, don't worry," she said. "Tonight. And I'll find out where she's hidden it, if it's the last thing I do!"

5

To Alex's fury, she had no chance to "get" Caroly that evening. Caroly made sure that she stayed in the same room as at least one of their parents until bedtime, and then she locked her bedroom door in case Alex had any ideas about coming for her in the middle of the night.

At midnight, Alex was still lying awake with her light on. As well as seething about Caroly, she was also worrying about the panto. The rehearsal today had been a complete disaster. Half the dwarfs' costumes didn't fit properly. Then Devi got dust in her nose and couldn't stop sneezing. Then Chaz forgot most of his lines. Then when the dance scene started, the dancers kept getting interrupted by weird noises from backstage: thumpings and slitherings and, once, an almighty crash. The crash was one of the pieces of scenery; it had been propped against a wall and had toppled over, breaking another, smaller piece in half as it fell.

Alex knew that the scenery hadn't fallen down by itself. It had been *pushed*. But they couldn't catch the culprit. Every time there was a noise they had all rushed backstage to investigate, and every time there was no one to be seen. Alex didn't need to guess who was behind the sabotage. Caroly's revolting little mates had decided to back up their threats with some action.

It was raining now; Alex could hear it pattering against her window. Someone's dog had started barking, too, and no one was doing anything to shut it up. Great! Fat chance she'd have of getting to sleep with that going on. Whose dog was it anyway? Not the Jenkins's or the Reeds'. And not that bad-tempered Labrador on the corner; he had a deep bark where this was a sharp, shrill yip-yelping.

In fact, it didn't *quite* sound like a dog at all. . .

Then, suddenly, something banged against the window.

Alex jumped as if she'd been shot – and a thought flashed into her mind: *Caroly!*

She leaped for the window and wrenched back the curtains, half expecting to see the glass broken and a stone or a clod of earth lying on the floor.

The window was intact. Apart from the rain streaming down, there was nothing there.

Except. . .

There was a mark on one of the panes. For a moment Alex thought it was a crack in the glass. But then she looked more closely.

It wasn't a crack. On the window pane, stuck to it by the rain, was a large brown feather.

That, Alex thought, explained the bang. A bird must have flown into the window, crashed against the glass and rebounded, leaving the feather behind. It happened sometimes; like that day when Dad had just hosed down the greenhouse. . .

The thought tailed off as it occurred to her that birds didn't fly around at midnight.

Except for owls, added her mind, wanting to be accurate.

And with a small, cold shiver she suddenly

remembered Mags's stuffed owl. The stuffed owl that she thought had blinked at her. . .

Alex let go of the curtains and went back to bed. It was stupid, of course. There was no possible connection between the stuffed owl and what had happened just now. The bang was probably just a gust of wind which had caught the feather and stuck it to the glass. She was letting Caroly's antics get to her, that was the trouble. *Get some sleep*, she told herself, *and stop being such a prat*.

The dog that didn't quite sound like a dog had stopped barking. Alex turned the light off, pulled the duvet over her head, and firmly shut her eyes.

With so many teachers around, Caroly was safe at school and she knew it. Alex saw her a few times during the day, and by the middle of the afternoon her sister was looking very smug. She was planning something else, Alex thought. Either that or she'd already done it. But what?

Alex found out when school was over and another rehearsal began. The fox-fur wrap was missing. And in its place in the costume cupboard was another note, this time demanding a ransom.

Mr Lawless was not amused. But he also had no intention of giving in to the eco-warriors' demands.

"We both know who's behind this," he said, looking daggers at Alex. "And it's got to stop. If you can't sort it out in a couple of days, I'll have to have a word with the Head. All right?"

"All right, Mr Lawless," Alex nodded, inwardly boiling. She'd get the truth out of Caroly. She'd *torture* it out of her, she thought, and enjoy every moment.

They were going to rehearse the big dance scene again today. It was a comic number, and all the dancers were got up in daft teddy bear costumes. Imogen Lawless had given Alex a lot of help with them, and as the scene began Alex took time off to watch.

This time there were no disruptions, and within a couple of minutes Alex was reduced to helpless giggles. Devi had a real comic talent. So What was lost in the forest at this point in the story, and her antics as she tried to grope her way out while the bears crept up on her were hilarious. The music was "The Teddy Bears' Picnic" – pretty inevitable, Alex thought; but it worked, and she found herself singing along.

"*If you go down to the woods today, you're sure of a big surprise. . .*" Alex's singing voice sounded like a hyaena with a sorrow, as Mr Lawless had once put it, and the nearest dancers gave her dirty looks as they heard her. But she didn't care.

"*If you go down to the woods today, you'd better not go alone*," she rasped cheerfully.

"Shut up, Alex!" grumbled a muffled voice from inside a bear costume.

Alex stuck her tongue out. "*It's lovely down in the woods today, but safer to stay at home! For—*"

She didn't get any further, because at that moment Devi uttered a yell of surprise. Alex turned her head just in time to see her skidding across the stage with arms windmilling madly; then her feet went from under her, she cannoned into three teddy bears and the whole lot of them crashed to the stage in a flailing, kicking heap.

People came running from all directions, and Mr Lawless and Squeak untangled the writhing muddle on stage and helped everyone to their feet.

"What *happened*?" asked Mr Lawless.

"I don't know!" Devi was breathless, brushing

herself down. "I was just doing that high kick – you know the one – when I felt something wrap round my leg. It tripped me up, then I skidded." She grimaced at the indignant teddy bears. "Sorry!"

Hands on hips, Mr Lawless stared around at the stage boards. "I can't see what could have caused it."

"Hold on," said Alex. "What's that?"

She pointed, and they all looked.

Lying at one side of the stage were Horrida's gloves, with their thumbs tied together.

"How the heck did *they* get there?" Mr Lawless was nonplussed. "Mags is supposed to be looking after these!" He turned round. "Mags! What d'you think you're doing, leaving your gloves lying around for Devi to trip over?"

"I didn't!" said Mags, appearing from behind the scenery. "I've just been looking for them; I put them back in the props box and someone took them out!"

Caroly, Alex thought darkly. But Caroly wasn't here; she hadn't dared show her face at rehearsal since the trouble with the eco-warriors began.

So who. . .?

"Ugh!" said Devi, rubbing a bruise on her knee. "No wonder they felt horrible when they touched me. I hate those gloves – they even *look* like snakes." She shuddered.

"Well, you don't have to wear them, do you?" Mags was ruffled because Mr Lawless had accused her of being careless when she knew she hadn't been. "I'll put them away. And when I get my hands on the joker who moved them. . ." She stalked off, still grumbling, as "The Teddy Bears' Picnic" bounced to an end.

"If you go down to the woods today, you're sure of a big surprise," said Alex with a grin. Then the grin faded as Mr Lawless gave her what Dad would have called a very old-fashioned look.

"OK," said Mr Lawless wearily. "Let's start again, shall we?"

Mags's mum was giving Alex a lift home, and Alex and Mags came out of the school to find that the rain had turned to a horrible, ice-cold sleet.

"Urrgh!" Mags pulled her coat collar up. "It's freezing! Come on, let's run!"

They pelted down the path, hunching against

the wind that drove the sleet into their faces, and piled into the car.

"Hi, Mrs Freeman!" said Alex. "Isn't the weather horrible?"

"Awful," Mrs Freeman agreed. "And it's going to get worse." She gestured at the car radio, which was on. "Snow, the forecast just said."

Mags groaned. "That's *all* we need!"

"Oh, I don't know." Alex looked sidelong at her and grinned wickedly. "I've got my repulsive sister to deal with, remember? If we get enough snow, maybe I can bury her in it, deep enough so no one'll ever find her!"

Arriving home, Alex prepared to do battle with Caroly. But the only person in the house was Dad, who greeted her worriedly.

"Caroly's at the hospital," he told her. "She had an accident – cut her hand really badly. Mum thought it might need stitching, so she's taken her to Casualty."

All Alex's plans to torture Caroly collapsed under sudden concern. Whatever she thought of her, Caroly was still her sister. "How did she do it?" she asked.

"I don't know. Broken glass or something,

she said – she was a bit shocked and there was a lot of blood, so we didn't hang around to ask questions. We'll find out more when they get back. They shouldn't be much longer."

They heard the car pull up half an hour later, and were in the hall when Mum shepherded Caroly in. Caroly's face was the colour of paper; she was shaky on her feet, and her right hand was swathed in a bandage.

"She had to have three stitches," Mum said anxiously. "And a tetanus shot, just in case."

Dad put an arm round Caroly's shoulders. "All right, love? Feeling a bit better?"

Caroly didn't answer. She was staring at Alex; then suddenly she said, "I want to go to bed."

"Of course, pet," soothed Mum. "I'll come and help you undress; you can't do much with that hand."

They went upstairs. Half way up, Caroly stopped and looked back at Alex again. There was an extraordinary expression on her face: a mixture of hostility and – bafflingly – fear. Then she turned and carried on towards the landing.

Next day the sleet had stopped, but it was bitterly cold and the heavy clouds had the pinky-purple tinge that heralded snow. Caroly didn't go to school. She was still shaky and in a strange, withdrawn mood, and, sitting alone on the bus, Alex did a lot of thinking.

There was something weird about Caroly's accident. To start with, neither she nor Mum nor Dad had been able to find out exactly how it had happened. Caroly had stuck to her story about broken glass – a toothbrush-tumbler in the bathroom, she said – and the pieces were there to prove it. But Mum had said that the wounds didn't look like glass cuts – in fact they didn't look like cuts at all. Caroly's fingers were *torn*. As the doctor at the hospital had said, it was just as if her hand had been bitten by a dog.

Caroly was lying about her injury; Alex would have bet a month's allowance on it. And she was certain that there was a connection with the eco-warriors' attempts to sabotage the panto.

The trouble was, what connection? Alex couldn't work it out. But the sympathy she had started to feel for her sister was vanishing rapidly. Somehow, she was going to find out the truth.

Her mind gnawed at the mystery all morning, like a dog gnawing a bone. Then, at lunchtime, Mags came looking for her.

"Come to the hall," Mags said urgently. "I've

got something to show you."

Mags looked worried, and Alex followed her to the school hall. Mags checked that no one else was around, then pointed to the costume cupboard.

"In there," she said in a low-pitched, dramatic voice. "Look."

Alex opened the cupboard door. At first she didn't know what Mags expected her to see. But then she did see it.

The fox-fur wrap was back, draped over a hanger on the rail. There was a dark stain around its muzzle, and when Alex reached out and touched it, her fingers came away sticky – and crimson.

The fox's glass eyes seemed to stare at her. The fox's face seemed to sneer. And from its mouth another drop of blood slowly formed, and fell to the floor with a faint *plink*.

6

"The one thing I can't work out," Mags said, "is how they did the blood. But the rest – well, it's all pretty obvious, isn't it?"

She and Alex were sitting on a pile of drapes behind the stage, finishing their sandwich-and-crisps lunches. Alex stared out at the deserted hall. She was seething again; all her fury with Caroly had come back, and what got to her most of all was the fact that her kid sister had made such fools of them.

She even had an explanation for the one thing Mags couldn't work out.

"It's Caroly's blood," she said, and told Mags about her sister's injured hand and the rush to

Casualty. Caroly must have cut herself deliberately, then smeared the fox's muzzle with her blood. Only she'd made a mistake, and the cut had been more serious than she'd intended. Then, when it wouldn't stop bleeding, she'd panicked and gone running to Mum, pretending that she'd had an accident.

"But how come the blood's still dripping?" Mags argued. "It should have congealed by now."

"Did you look *inside* the fox's mouth?" Alex asked her.

"No. . ."

"Well, I think we should. And I bet we'll find the remains of a plastic bag or something."

"You mean, she put some blood in a bag, so that it would drip and . . . *yuk*!" Mags pulled a face. "That's *disgusting*."

"My sister *is* disgusting," Alex said with feeling. "Come on; let's see if I'm right."

She was. The fox's mouth was hinged to make it look more realistic, and when Alex fished cautiously inside it, she found several shreds of what looked like cling film.

"There!" she said triumphantly. "What did I tell you?"

Mags peered at the shreds. "It *looks* like plastic," she agreed. "The only thing is. . ."

"What?" Alex frowned.

Mags prodded one of the bits with a tentative finger. "It doesn't *feel* like plastic." She thought back to a recent biology lesson, and suddenly started to feel a little bit sick. "It's more like . . . *skin*."

"Skin?" Alex echoed. "Oh, come on! It's just gone funny, that's all. Cling film always does once it's been used, doesn't it?"

"I suppose so," said Mags doubtfully.

"Well, we've solved the mystery." Alex was pleased with herself. "And the way Caroly's trick backfired has given her a serious fright." She took the fox fur down from the hanger. "I'll clean this up before lessons start. We've got art this afternoon – I think we can tell Mr Lawless that we won't be having any more trouble from the eco-warriors!"

"What about the stag's head, though?" said Mags. "We still haven't found that."

Alex grinned. "I reckon it'll come back – mysteriously, and all by itself. Bet you a Snickers bar?"

Mags laughed. "No way! I'd lose."

They left the hall, shutting the door behind them. When they had gone, everything was silent . . . until, behind the stage, the door of the costume cupboard creaked. There was no one there to hear it. And no one to see when slowly, almost cautiously, it swung open. Just as if somebody was pushing it from the inside. Only of course there *was* nobody inside. There were just the costumes: the outfits on their hangers and the hats on a shelf above.

Then one of the hats moved slightly. As if, again, someone had pushed it. Horrida's hat. It slid to the edge of the shelf, wobbled . . . tipped . . . and fell to the floor. Two feathers came off, and a chilly little draught sent them skittering across the floor. They fetched up against the stacked scenery flats and stayed there, fluttering gently.

From behind the stack of flats came an odd noise, almost like a rustling.

Then everything was still.

Fat, white flakes started to drift past the window during the art lesson, and by the time school ended, snow was falling heavily.

"Great!" Mags groaned as she and Alex got their coats. "You know what that means, don't you? All the boys'll be waiting in ambush with snowballs! That's all I need!"

"We could hang on till they get bored and go

home," Alex suggested. "Catch the later bus. Tell you what – I want to take some costume bits back to work on. Come to the hall and help me sort them out, and that'll kill the time."

The hall was empty and the lights off. Dusk was already gathering outside and the snow made the day gloomier still. Alex shivered as she fumbled for the light switches.

"It's *cold* in here! The heating must have gone wrong again. Oh, blast, and the big light isn't working!"

"The tube's gone," said Mags. "It was flickering this morning. Just put the stage lights on; we don't need the main ones anyway."

Alex pressed another switch. At the end of the hall, half hidden behind the pushed-back stage curtains, two bulbs lit up, casting a dim glow over the stage.

The stage should have been empty. But it wasn't.

"What the—" said Alex.

"I don't believe it. . ." said Mags.

Piled in a heap in the middle of the stage were half the contents of the costume cupboard and props box. Even from here the girls could see the stuffed owl, Horrida's hat and handbag, the "magic" mirror, and the curtains from the boudoir scene.

And perched on top of the chaotic assortment was the missing stag's head.

Alex got to the stage first and scrambled up. She reached for the stag's head, wanting to see if it was damaged.

The stag's fur was sopping wet. So were the owl's feathers. And when she picked up the mock-croc handbag, a dollop of half-melted snow fell out of it.

Mags, puffing up behind her, said rather obviously, "Everything's *soaked*!" She fingered the curtains. "These, too! Looks like your sister's been at it again."

"No." Alex stared down at the jumble. "Caroly's at home. This time it can't have been her."

"Well, her friends, then. Oh, *no*! Half the feathers have come off my hat, look! And there's bits of fur all over the place; they must be from the gloves, and they're all draggled and messed up!"

"I don't think it was her friends, either," said Alex.

"Well, who else would do it?"

Alex shook her head. "I mean, they *couldn't*. Remember when the stag was stolen? Mr

Lawless locked the props box. And he's the only person with a key. So how did they get this stuff out?"

"They must have forced the lock!" Mags was starting to get angry, which was very rare for her. "I'm going to look."

She marched off behind-stage. There was some thumping and banging, then a grunt. . .

And then a piercing yell.

"Mags?" Alex felt her heart turn over. She started for the backstage area. Now she could hear the sounds of a scuffle, and as she ran round the edge of the wings, two figures lurched out of the gloom and cannoned into her.

They tripped over each other's legs, and all three of them fell over. Sitting up dazedly, Alex found herself staring at Chaz Peterson.

"Chaz! Whatever are *you* doing here?"

"Look at his hair!" Mags yelled, scrambling to her feet. "It's wet, just like all the stuff on the stage! He's the one trying to wreck our panto!"

Chaz's jaw dropped. "*Me?* Don't be so daft! I'm *in* the panto – why would I want to wreck it?"

"Well, what were you doing?" Mags demanded.

Chaz bit his lip. "I . . . er. . ."

"See?" said Mags triumphantly. "He can't explain!"

"I can!" Chaz argued. "But if I did, you. . ." He looked at them helplessly, then his shoulders sagged. "You wouldn't believe me. You just wouldn't."

"Try us," Alex said. There was suddenly a serious note in her voice, and it silenced Mags, who had been about to start shouting again.

"Well . . . me and some of the guys, we thought we'd have a bit of fun with the snow. You know. . ."

"Ambushing all the girls with snowballs," said Mags darkly. "Yeah. We know your idea of fun!"

"All *right*! Listen, will you? We were round the back of the canteen, and I saw these footprints. In the snow."

"Big deal," Mags interrupted again. "So someone was there before you."

"No," said Chaz. "Not someone. Some*thing*. An animal – but not a bird, or a dog or cat, or anything I've ever seen before. These prints were *big*. So I followed them. And they led here."

"*Here?*" Mags was scornful. "How could

they? There's no snow in here to show them up."

"I know," Chaz said. "But they . . . well, they led to the skylight. On the roof."

The girls stared at him for maybe a minute. Chaz's face was turning red; he shuffled his feet and wouldn't look up.

At last Alex broke the silence. "I think," she said, "we'd better see this."

Chaz led the way as they headed for the outside door. Alex had the feeling that he was *glad* they'd found him. Whatever he had really discovered out there, he badly wanted someone else to know about it, too. For once, Chaz wasn't playing a practical joke, and that gave Alex a queasy sensation in her stomach that she didn't like at all.

Outside, the snow was still falling, though less heavily. It was really dusk now; the snowballers had gone, and everything was very quiet. Chaz led them eagerly to the back of the hall, then stopped as he realized that there was a layer of fresh snow over everything.

"It's covered them!" he said in dismay. "But they were there – I swear they were!"

"You know what?" said Mags to Alex, "I think our dear friend Chaz has been winding us up."

"Wait a minute." Alex blinked snow out of her eyes. "What's that, over there?"

Just visible under the new snow was a faint trail. They went to look more closely.

"They *are* footprints," said Mags. "But anything could have made them."

"They're not human." Alex's voice was tense. "Look at them. Look at that shape."

The prints were very broad and flat, and each one had a semicircle of distinct points, as if claws had dug deeper into the snow. But no animal Alex had ever seen had feet that big. They seemed . . . *prehistoric*, she thought. And, as Chaz had said, the trail led to the school hall.

She looked up at the hall roof –

And her heart nearly stopped.

The snow on the roof lay more thinly than the snow on the ground. And the strange footprints continued. They led straight as an arrow up the roof's sloping side, then, at the edge of the skylight, they ended.

Very slowly, Alex and Mags turned to look at each other.

"Oh my God," said Mags. "What *is* it?"

Alex glanced in Chaz's direction. For one moment she thought – hoped – that she would see a sly grin on his face, and that this whole thing was a wind-up as Mags had first suspected. But Chaz wasn't grinning. His expression was deadly serious.

And *scared*.

She swallowed, horribly aware that she was frightened too. The footprints stopped at the skylight, but the skylight was tightly closed. So where had it – whatever it was – gone?

"It couldn't have got into the hall." Mags's voice was shaky. "Could it. . .?"

Alex licked her lips. "We'd better go and look," she said, trying to sound braver than she felt. "Come on."

They hurried back inside. They could hear the caretaker in the distance; he'd begun locking up, so they wouldn't have much time for a search. Where to start? Alex thought nervously. They didn't even know what they were looking for.

However, they found the first clue almost immediately – a small puddle of water directly underneath the closed skylight. Melted snow? The props and costumes heaped on the stage were wet, too. There *had* to be a connection. But what?

"The costume cupboard door's open," said

Mags. "But the props box is still locked. How could that stuff have been got out?"

Chaz looked round uneasily. "You don't think it could be Mr Lawless, do *you*? I mean, he *has* got the key."

"Mr Lawless is a bit crazy, but he's not barking mad," Alex said firmly. "And if he was going to set something up to scare off the eco-warriors, he'd have told us. I think we ought to—"

She stopped in mid-sentence as a loud scraping noise came from the direction of the stage. For an instant the three of them froze – then, as one, they ran to investigate.

The stage was just as they had left it. Nothing moved; there was no sound. Baffled, they stared around.

Then the scraping noise came again.

It was coming from under the boards.

"What *is* it. . .?" Mags whispered. But Chaz made a shushing gesture. He tiptoed across the stage and down the steps at the side.

"Chaz, what are you doing?" Mags hissed. Chaz shushed again, and pointed to the gap behind the steps. You could get underneath the stage from there, and Mags's eyes widened in alarm.

"Chaz, *don't*!"

Chaz took no notice. They saw him disappear under the stage. They heard his feet scuffling, then a muffled swear word as he stubbed his toe in the darkness.

Then. . .

It wasn't a scraping this time. It was a rushing, crashing, thunderous noise, as if something huge was charging through the clutter of struts under the stage boards. They heard Chaz's gasp of horror. Then his voice rose up in a shriek of pure terror that dinned in their ears and echoed through the hall:

"Aaah! NO! *NOOOO!*"

7

Chaz exploded from under the stage like a bullet out of a gun. Alex saw his face as he hurled himself across the hall. It was the face of someone whose worst nightmare had just come appallingly to life. From beneath her feet came a grinding crash, then a roar. The stage boards bucked and shook; Mags screamed at the top of her voice and leaped backwards, barrelling into Alex and sending her tottering. Alex flailed her arms to regain her balance, and her voice rang shrilly through the hall.

"*Chaz! CHAZ!*"

Chaz didn't even pause. Legs pumping desperately, he was running for the door. Alex jumped down the steps after him – but as she reached the bottom, her foot caught in something and she was sent flying, measuring her length on the floor with a thump that knocked the breath out of her. As she raised her head dizzily, she was in time to see the door smacking back on its hinges as Chaz barged through and out of the hall.

Alex's feet were tangled in something. She scrabbled to get it off, then saw that it was the strap of the handbag from Horrida's costume. Whatever was it doing *there*? But there was no time to think of that now. She had to catch Chaz!

She jumped up and ran. Mags was following, Alex could hear her shouting, but she didn't wait. Outside, the snow was like a blizzard, and the security light had come dazzlingly on as Chaz tore past. Struggling to see through the glare, she peered into the gathering dark, but Chaz had gone.

"Alex!" Mags caught her up, panting. "Did you see where he went?"

"No! We've got to find him, Mags!"

"Look!" Mags cried, pointing. "New footprints!"

She was right. A single trail led away across the school grounds. Deep prints, like the marks of someone racing.

Suddenly a voice shouted from behind them. "Hey, you! What's going on out here? What was that screaming?"

"It's the caretaker!" Alex hissed. "Come on – *run*!"

They pelted away into the flying snow, following Chaz's tracks, and didn't slow down until they were sure the caretaker wouldn't be able to see them.

"Oh, Alex!" Mags gasped. "Wait for me – I've got to get my breath back!"

Alex stopped, and stared through the snow to get her bearings. They were almost at the edge of the school grounds now. The boundary was marked by a privet hedge, looming white in the darkness, and beyond that was the local park. Chaz's footprints zigzagged right up to the hedge, and broken twigs littered the ground where he'd reached it. He must have charged straight through, Alex thought.

Then she saw the *other* marks in the snow.

They were the same shape as the marks that they'd seen on the hall roof. Wide, flat, and *clawed*. They led in a straight line, following Chaz's tracks. In fact they'd been following them all the way from the hall.

Though there was nothing but the prints to be seen, the logic of it was horribly obvious.

They weren't the only ones pursuing Chaz. Something else was chasing him too. . .

"Come on," Alex said to Mags, who was recovering. "We've got to keep following!"

"To the park?" Mags looked at her in horror. "But those tracks. . ."

Alex was no less scared, but she fought the fear with all her strength. "We've *got* to!" she repeated. "We can't just leave Chaz out there. And there's two of us – if we stick together, it'll be OK."

Mags wasn't convinced. But she wasn't about to let Alex go alone, either. There was a gate in the hedge, which Chaz had been too terrified to even think of using. They let themselves out of the grounds and started towards the park.

"At least there are some lights," Mags said quaveringly, looking at the decorative street-lamps that marked the park's pathways. "Though I'd give anything for a torch. . ."

Alex didn't answer. She was too busy concentrating on trying to follow Chaz's tracks in the dark. When they reached the lamps, she thought, it would be easier. Unless Chaz had taken off across the grass. . .

They paused again when they came to the first lamp. Chaz's prints went straight past it. But the other prints, the clawed ones, didn't. They simply *stopped*. Ended. As if whatever made them had reached a certain point, then vanished into thin air.

"How. . .?" Mags began wonderingly, but she couldn't finish the question because it didn't make any sense.

Alex stared at the prints in confusion. Then something occurred to her.

"They stop where the lamp is. See? There's a circle of light on the snow, and the last print's right on the edge of it."

"What could that mean? That it isn't real? It's a – a ghost?"

"I don't know. But at least it's not chasing Chaz any more. Come *on*, Mags. We're losing time!"

They set off on Chaz's trail again. At first the tracks stayed on the path, as Alex had hoped. But after a while, the path curved – and the tracks didn't.

The girls tried to keep following the prints, but after a few metres they realized it was hopeless. Without the lamps to help them, it was too dark to see the footprints unless they got down on their hands and knees.

"We can't crawl after him," Alex said in dismay.

Mags agreed. "It's hopeless. We're not going to find him."

They tried shouting Chaz's name, but the only answer was the eerie hoot of an owl in a tree some way off. Mags shivered at the sound, thinking of all the horror movies she'd ever seen, and looked back longingly at the lamps on their tall posts.

"We ought to tell someone," she said nervously.

Alex shook her head. "No. Chaz's house is over there, isn't it? On the other side of the park. The tracks are heading that way. I think he's running home."

"But will he get there?" asked Mags.

They looked at each other but neither tried to answer the question. At last Alex said, "If he's not in school tomorrow morning, we *will* tell someone. Till then, I think we should wait."

Mags shivered again. "We've missed both the school buses."

"We'll get an ordinary one outside the park gates." Alex peered into the gathering night one last time, then sighed, and they turned together and began to hurry back along the path.

They weren't very far from the gates, huddling into their coats against the snow, when Mags said:

"Alex . . . can you *hear* something?"

Alex's stomach gave a queasy little lurch. "Such as. . .?"

"I'm not sure. A sort of . . . rustling."

So Mags had noticed it, too. Alex wished she hadn't. She had just about managed to convince herself that it was only her imagination, or maybe some trick of the falling snow. Now, in a moment, all her hard work melted away.

The truth was, she had been aware of the noise for the past five minutes. And whatever was making it was following them.

"At the next lamp," she said, keeping her voice down, "we'll take a look, OK?"

"OK."

They drew level with the lamp, and halted. The rustling stopped, too. It occurred to Alex that this was horribly like the incident in the school grounds on Sunday evening. Only this time, it couldn't possibly be Caroly or her friends.

"Who's going to be first to look back?"

Mags asked apprehensively.

Alex took a deep breath and turned her head.

As far as she could see, the dark path behind them was deserted.

Then, under a clump of bushes, a shadow moved.

"*Alex!*" Mags squeaked. She grabbed Alex's arm, nearly pulling her off balance. The shadow froze. Then it moved again, fast. It stretched . . . and suddenly resolved into the shape of a rabbit, that darted across the path and dived into another bush on the opposite side. The bush rustled, with exactly the same sound that had spooked them.

Alex and Mags stood open-mouthed and feeling totally foolish.

"A *rabbit*." Mags didn't know whether to laugh or cry. "A harmless little *rabbit*! What a pair of idiots we are!"

Alex had started to giggle and had trouble stopping. "Let's get going," she said at last, linking her arm through Mags's. "Before we get double pneumonia!"

Still giggling, they swung round.

And with a clattering, whirring racket, something huge erupted out of a holly tree beside the path and hurtled straight at their heads.

"*Aaagh!*" Mags's scream echoed Alex's as they both staggered backwards, flinging their arms up to ward off the flying terror. There was a rush of air, a noise like a mini-thunderclap, and the black silhouette swooped past them. Through a mayhem of snow and her own terror, Alex glimpsed sweeping wings, round, glaring eyes, and heard a hooting, shivering cry that rang eerily through the park. Then her feet went from under her and she and Mags crashed to the ground together.

As the silhouette sped away, they picked themselves up. They were both shaking from head to foot and their hearts pounded with shock. The dark shape was still just visible against the sky, flying towards the wood at the far side of the park. They stared after it until it vanished, then Mags let out her breath in a groan.

"Oh my God! I don't think I've ever been so frightened in my life!" And when Alex didn't reply she added cheeringly, "Hey, it's all right! It wasn't really anything to be scared of. It was just an owl."

"Yeah . . . OK," said Alex. *Just an owl. Again. . .*

She didn't say another word, but started

towards the park gates at a run. She wanted very badly to get home.

Because, suddenly, home seemed like the only place left that was safe.

8

Alex spent a wakeful night of gnawing worry. To Mum and Dad's astonishment she was up an hour before her usual time, and caught the early bus to school. Caroly was still at home. She had refused to speak to Alex at all last night, but at the moment Caroly was the last thing Alex cared about. She was desperate to know what had become of Chaz.

It was a while before she found out because when she got to school, two things had happened to grab everyone's attention.

First, the caretaker had found the pile of wet things on the stage, and he had reported it to Mr Lawless. Mr Lawless was as puzzled as anyone else. The key to the props box hadn't left his pocket, and the lock hadn't been forced. Yet somehow the box had been opened. It was a mystery, and all the bright ideas from half the panto cast didn't help to solve it.

Second, there were the footprints in the grounds.

It had stopped snowing at about ten p.m. and there had been no more falls since. And in the fresh white blanket around the school buildings were tracks – literally hundreds of them – and not one made by a human foot. Birds? Well, fair enough, everyone said; the younger kids had a bird table and put out food in winter. But a lot of the bird tracks were far too big to be the usual sparrows or blackbirds or robins. Then there were the pawprints. The Head, who was keen on wildlife, recognized rabbits, foxes, badgers and even the slotted hoof marks of deer – doubly astonishing, as there *were* no deer in the area so far as anyone knew.

And to add further to the confusion, there were some very large prints that no one could recognize at all.

At least, no one except Alex and Mags.

They looked for Chaz but couldn't find him. Then, at registration, they found out that

Chaz's elder brother had brought a note from their mum. Chaz had a bad cold, and wouldn't be coming to school today.

"At least we know he got home safely," Alex whispered to Mags.

"Yes. But a "bad cold" – bad fright's more like it. And he wasn't the only one!"

There was to be another rehearsal after school, and Alex shuddered as she thought back to last night and to how it had started. What had happened to Chaz underneath the stage? What had terrified him?

What had been lurking under there?

She only hoped and prayed that, when the rehearsal began, they weren't going to find out.

Alex and Mags waited until everyone else was in the hall for the rehearsal before they ventured through the doors. They approached the stage in trepidation – Alex could feel her heart bumping against her ribs – but everything appeared to be normal, and when they rushed up the steps nothing pounced out to attack them. Devi Gupta gave them an odd look but said nothing, and Alex and Mags tried to forget their terrors and concentrate.

Mr Lawless was not in a good mood. He had

had a 'phone call that afternoon from Chaz's mum, and it had brought bad news.

"Chaz has pulled out of the panto," he told the rest of the cast exasperatedly. "Just like that. No reason, no explanation – he simply doesn't want to do it."

"Stage fright," someone commented smugly. "Chaz the Chicken!"

"Maybe, maybe not." Mr Lawless glowered around at them all. "But whatever the truth, it doesn't help us. Our big night's a week tomorrow! Robbie, you're Chaz's understudy. Do you reckon you can take over in the time we've got?"

Robbie Blake grinned. "You bet, Mr Lawless! My big chance, isn't it?"

Alex groaned inwardly. Where Chaz was tall and thin, Robbie was short and podgy. She'd have to put in hours of extra work, altering Chaz's costume.

Then she remembered something, and said hopefully, "But Mr Lawless, Robbie's doing the voices for the mirror and the animals, isn't he? He won't be able to manage both, so maybe someone else ought to—"

She had been going to finish, "ought to play the Fairy Godfather", but Mr Lawless interrupted.

"Good point, Alex. All right; since you thought of it, you can do the backstage voices instead."

"*Me?*" Alex's jaw dropped.

"Yes. Why not? You're quite a good mimic; you'll probably do it better than Robbie anyway."

"But—" Alex began. Then stopped as she realized that she couldn't explain to Mr Lawless why she very much did *not* want to be the voice of the owl and the stag. Mr Lawless would say she was inventing excuses and tell her not to be so silly. He simply wouldn't believe the truth.

She knew that Mags was looking at her, and could imagine the expression on her face. Avoiding looking back, she nodded, her heart sinking.

"All right, Mr L. I'll do it."

"That's the stuff!" said Mr Lawless, sounding much more cheerful. "Never say die, eh?"

"What?" Alex's head came up sharply.

He smiled. "Just one of my proverbs. Who knows? This might be your big break, too!"

Or the biggest mistake I've ever made in my life, thought Alex.

* * *

"*'Mirror, mirror, on the wall,*
WHO is the fairest of them all?' "

There was silence for a few moments. Then Mr Lawless's voice hissed irritably, "Alex! Wake up back there!"

Alex, who had been staring nervously at the floorboards since the scene began, jumped and shook her mind out of its paralysis. "Sorry!" she whispered. "Er. . ." A rustling of papers as she looked for the right place in her script. "Oh, yes . . . er. . .

'Horrida, in your fur and feather,
You're Queen of Evil altogether!
But though you dress up like a zoo,
So What is fairer far than you!' "

"OK," said Mr Lawless. "It's not exactly Shakespeare, but blame the scriptwriters, not me. Right, Horrida; let's hear that screech of rage – and try not to have a coughing fit this time!"

Mags let out a fearsome yell that made Alex jump again. "Great!" said Mr Lawless. "But you keep forgetting to stamp your foot."

"Um . . . do you think the stamping really

works, Mr Lawless?" said Mags. "I mean, with these heels on, if I fell over—"

"You haven't fallen over once in two months of rehearsals. Come on, Mags, what's the matter with you all of a sudden?"

Mags mumbled, "Nothing." There was a pause, then the boards shook as she thumped her heel down on them. Alex cringed, shutting her eyes. But there was no answering roar from below, no crashing and bashing as something weird and horrible came whirling out from under the stage to attack them.

Alex told herself to stop being so stupid. There couldn't possibly be anything hiding down there. *No, of course not*, said an inner voice. *Nothing at all. That's why Chaz is so terrified that he's pulled out of the panto.*

Oh, shut up! she told the voice ferociously. There wasn't anything. There couldn't be. She and Mags had imagined it.

Sure, said the inner voice. *And you imagined the footprints on the roof. And the ones that followed Chaz into the park. And all those other tracks in the grounds this morning.*

The trouble was, she thought miserably, however mad the whole thing seemed, it *had* been more than imagination. And if there really was some hidden horror under the stage, they couldn't just ignore it and hope it would go away. Something had to be done.

But what *did* you do about a thing like that?

"Al-*EX!*" Mr Lawless's voice bawled out and she nearly jumped out of her skin yet again. "Will you concentrate! Next line – the owl's dialogue!"

Alex scrabbled for the script. Owl, owl . . . got it! Now, Mags had just thrown a tantrum, shouting, "*Who is the fairest? Who, who, WHO?*"

"'*Too-wit, too-woo!*'" hooted Alex sepulchrally. "'*Not yoooou! So poooh!*'"

Stiletto heels clicked across the stage, and the flat in front of Alex shook slightly as Mags grabbed hold of the stuffed owl on the other side.

"'*You wretched, round-eyed, dimwit bird!*'" she recited, sounding as if she was thoroughly enjoying this bit, "'*Such rubbish I have never heard! I'll pull your feathers, pluck your eyes, and cook what's left in a big owl'* – OW!"

There was a thud of something being dropped, and then Mr Lawless's voice, "Mags? What's up?"

"My arm!" Mags wailed. "Oooh, that *hurt!*"

With a horrible sense of foreboding, Alex rushed round to the front of the stage.

The stuffed owl lay on its back on the floor, looking faintly ridiculous with its legs stuck up in the air. Mags had pushed her sleeve up and was staring at a long red scratch on her forearm.

And on one of the owl's talons was a scarlet bead of blood.

"You must have caught your arm on the claw when you picked it up," said Mr Lawless. "Let's have a look. Oh, it's not serious. Better put a bit of antiseptic on it, though. There'll be some in the First Aid cupboard."

"I'll go with her, Mr L," said Alex quickly. "Come on, Mags, let's get you patched up." She saw that Devi was looking strangely at her again, but was too preoccupied to wonder about it as she hurried Mags away.

As soon as they were out of earshot of the stage Alex said urgently, "What *really* happened?"

Mags shot a nervous glance back over her shoulder. "It scratched me," she said tersely. "I mean, it *moved*, Alex. I *saw* it. That thing *moved*!"

"I believe you." Alex's voice was grim.

"Mags, we've got to get together and talk about this. There's something very deeply weird going on, and I—"

She stopped as Mags nudged her warningly. Then she heard the quick footsteps behind them.

"Are you all right, Mags?" It was Devi. She looked from one to the other of them, searchingly. "Can I help?"

"No," said Alex, more sharply than she'd intended. "Thanks."

"It's nothing to worry about." Mags faked a smile. "We'll be back in a minute."

As they reached the First Aid cupboard Mags whispered, "She hasn't gone away. She's hanging around."

"I know. *Why*?"

"Maybe she suspects something?"

"There isn't anything to suspect. Not anything sane, anyway. Unless. . ." Alex's voice tailed off.

"Unless what?" prompted Mags.

Alex glanced covertly back at Devi. She was pretending to study some pictures on the corridor wall, but Alex wasn't fooled. Devi was watching them very closely. And she was worried.

Alex turned back to Mags and put her mouth close to her ear. "Unless," she whispered, "there was something else about that business with the gloves. Something Devi hasn't told us. . .?"

9

"There she goes." Mags pointed along the road outside the school. About fifty metres ahead, Devi was walking towards the town bus stop. "Come on – before we lose our nerve!"

They started to run. As they approached, Devi heard them, turned, and stopped.

"Hi!" she said. "Anything wrong?"

She definitely *did* look worried, Alex thought. Aloud, she said, "We could ask you the same question."

"Oh?" Devi smiled. "I don't understand."

"We think you do," Mags put in with a rush. "Only you don't want to admit it. Just like us." Meaningfully, she held up her scratched arm.

"Ah. . ." said Devi. "Then there *was* something funny about it. I thought so."

"Yeah, we noticed. You weren't exactly subtle, Dev. Look, can we make a deal? Tell us what's happened to you, and we'll tell you what happened to us."

Devi stared down at the pavement. "You'll laugh."

"Oh, no," said Alex. "We won't."

The serious note in her voice got through Devi's doubts. "All right," she said after a pause. "But not here."

"Why not?"

"Because. . ." She glanced edgily at the snow-shrouded hedge of the front garden by which they were standing. "Just not here, all right? I'd rather go somewhere where there aren't any bushes."

Aha! thought Alex. Aloud, she said, "Let's all go to my house. Mum and Dad won't mind – and there certainly aren't any bushes in my bedroom!"

Devi laughed, but nervously. "Fine," she said.

Alex had forgotten that her parents were going out that evening. That was a bonus, because it would give them the house to themselves. Caroly would be there, of course. But if Alex's growing suspicion was right, that might be just as well.

Devi had been very uneasy on the walk from the bus stop to the house. She kept to the road side of the pavement, away from front gardens, and she kept looking back over her shoulder, as if she half expected something to be following them. Once they were indoors, though, she visibly relaxed. Mum had left a casserole in the oven and generously told them all to help themselves. Caroly didn't appear, though Alex had seen her bedroom curtains twitch as they walked up the path. So she knew they were here, and she was keeping out of the way.

When Mum and Dad had gone, the three of them went to Alex's room.

"Right," Alex said to Devi. "So why were you so interested when Mags's arm got scratched this afternoon?"

Devi opened her mouth to say, "I wasn't," then changed her mind. She sighed.

"This *is* going to sound crazy, but . . . when it happened, I thought I saw the owl's claw *move*."

"It did," said Mags.

Devi stared. Then: "Has anything . . . else happened to you two?" she asked.

"Anything *else*?" Mags glanced at Alex and gave a hollow laugh. "Let's tell her the lot, Alex. You start."

Devi listened with wide, serious eyes as they told her the whole story. When she heard what had happened to Chaz, she let out a low whistle.

"No *wonder* he's pulled out of the panto! But the thing that chased him – you didn't see it?"

"No," said Alex. "Only the footprints. The same ones that were on the hall roof."

"Wait a minute," Mags put in. "This morning, at school – remember those tracks in the snow? The ones even the Head couldn't recognize? They were the same, too."

Devi gasped and sat bolt upright. "*Those?*" There was horror in her voice.

"Yes. Why? Do you know anything about them?"

Devi nodded. "Y-yes. I've seen tracks like them before."

"Whyever didn't you say so this morning?"

"Because no one would have believed me. Now, though. . ." She swallowed. "Mum and Dad took me for a holiday to India last year. We stayed with my Aunty, and while we were there we went on a trip to one of the National Parks.

I saw some tracks exactly like the ones at school this morning, and one of the park rangers told me what made them."

She stopped. "Well, go on!" Alex prompted. "What *did* make them?"

Devi looked back very steadily.

"A crocodile," she said.

Alex's mouth opened, but nothing came out. Mags just goggled.

"I know," continued Devi helplessly. "It's completely mad, isn't it? But I swear that's what those tracks are."

Alex felt a hideous, cold sensation forming in the pit of her stomach. When she had run after Chaz last night, something had tripped her up. Horrida's handbag, which only minutes before had been on the stage, had somehow got itself to the foot of the steps, just where Chaz had burst out. The handbag. The mock-crocodile handbag.

Or *was* it mock-crocodile?

Could it just – could it possibly, be *real*?

Then Devi said something that blotted the train of thought right out of her mind.

"I wouldn't have believed it myself, I don't think, if it hadn't been for the snake."

"*Snake?*" Alex and Mags yelped in unison.

Devi nodded. "Remember what happened at rehearsal on Wednesday, when those awful gloves somehow got on to the stage and I tripped over them?"

"Yes," said Mags. "And I didn't put them there, whatever Mr Lawless thinks."

"I know you didn't. And I'll tell you how I know." Devi licked her lips nervously. "I was late getting away from the rehearsal. Nearly everyone else had gone, and there was just me and Squeak – Miss Macey – left. I was putting some of my costume stuff away. I opened the cupboard door and something moved, down on the floor. I pulled back one of the cloaks to have a look, and – and a *snake* shot out." She shuddered. "I just *screamed*. Squeak came running and I told her. The snake had gone behind one of the scenery flats. She got a stick and went to look. You know what she found?"

Alex and Mags shook their heads. They'd had no idea that Squeak was so brave.

"One of those gloves," said Devi.

"You mean—" Alex began.

"I mean there was no sign of a snake; there was just the glove," said Devi. "Squeak thought I'd been winding her up; she really had a go at me. But I know what I saw. And the glove couldn't have got there by itself, could it?"

"Alex," said Mags hollowly, "what are those gloves made of?"

Horribly, chillingly, Alex was thinking exactly the same thing.

"I don't know," she replied. "But I know what they look like."

Snake skin. That was what they looked like. Devi had seen a snake. And the stuffed owl had blinked at Alex and clawed Mags. And the handbag had been under the stage, where *something* was lying in wait for Chaz.

"Maybe it was the eco-warriors," Devi said uneasily. "Maybe they rigged all these things up somehow. I mean, there's got to be a *sensible* explanation, hasn't there?"

"The eco-warriors are Year Sevens, not magicians!" Alex retorted. Then, thinking of the Year Sevens, she remembered Caroly's "accident". The doctor at the hospital had said that her hand looked as if it had been attacked by a dog. . .

She got up and started across the room. "Hang on a minute," she said. "I've just had an idea."

She reached the door, opened it – and was

just in time to see Caroly fleeing to her own bedroom.

"Come back here, you!" Alex sprinted after her sister and barged into her room before she could shut the door. Grabbing her by both arms she demanded, "How long have you been out there listening?"

"I wasn't!" Caroly protested. "Oww! Mind my hand!"

"I'll mash the other one if I don't get some answers!" Alex snarled. "Mags, Devi – come and help me!"

Between the three of them they dragged Caroly back to Alex's room. With assorted threats they made her confess that she had eavesdropped on their whole conversation, and the look on her face as she admitted it told Alex that she was as scared as they were.

"All right," said Alex at last. "Suppose you tell us what *really* happened to your hand?"

No answer. Caroly hunched her shoulders and stared at the carpet.

"You took the fox fur, didn't you?" Mags added. "And you made up the ransom note."

A shrug. "So what if I did?"

Alex sighed exasperatedly. "So, what *happened* when you took it? Come on, Caroly!

We think we know anyway."

"Then you don't need me to tell you, do you?"

Alex clenched her fist, but Devi said, "Just a minute, Alex: Listen Caroly. There's something very weird going on, and we need to find out as much as we can. Otherwise, next time someone might get very badly hurt – or even killed."

Caroly looked up at her. "Killed?"

"Maybe. We don't know. That's why we need your help."

There was a long silence. Then, in a very small voice, Caroly said,

"It bit me."

Alex and Mags exchanged a look that said, *Thought so!* "Tell us about it," said Alex quietly.

The story came out at last. Caroly had taken the fur from the costume cupboard and brought it home to hide it in her room. It still smelled a bit, so she took it into the bathroom, planning to sprinkle it with some talcum powder to sweeten it up. She was just about to shake the talc over the fur when suddenly it squirmed in her hand. And before she could react in any way at all, the fox's head twisted round, and a mouthful of teeth ripped into her fingers.

"I didn't believe it," Caroly said, her voice shaky now. "I thought I'd dreamed it. But then

I saw all the blood. And it hurt *incredibly*. . ."

She had flung the fox fur away from her and stood staring at it, helpless with shock and terror. But whatever strange power had brought the fox to life had vanished as suddenly as it had come. It was just an old fur wrap again, with glass eyes and no teeth.

Caroly's hand was in a bad way, but she couldn't tell Mum and Dad the truth, of course. So she had smashed the toothbrush-glass and pretended to have cut herself on the pieces. She kicked the fox fur into the airing cupboard and left it there. She was much too frightened to touch it again.

"Hold on," said Alex when she heard this. "So how did you get it back to school?"

Caroly frowned. "I didn't. It's still in the airing cupboard."

"Wrong," said Mags. "It's in the costume cupboard. I found it there myself. With blood on it."

Caroly looked bewildered. "But it can't be. . ."

She and Alex both jumped to their feet and ran to the bathroom. Mags and Devi followed in time to see Alex open the airing cupboard door.

"It's gone!" Caroly whispered. Her face was dead white and she looked as if she was going to be sick. "But how? It can't have *walked*!"

"Can't it?" said Alex. The horrible thought she had had earlier was creeping back. The owl. The fox. The bag. All those tracks in the snow.

And Chaz. . .

"They're coming alive," she said in a small, fearful voice. "The animals in our props and costume bits . . . They're *all* coming alive!"

10

"Alex, that's completely nuts!" Mags protested.

"I know," said Alex hollowly. "But has anyone got a better explanation?"

They hadn't; she could see it in their faces. Her theory was impossible, but the facts were staring straight at them.

Caroly's lower lip began to tremble, and suddenly she wasn't a daring and passionate eco-warrior any more but just Alex's kid sister.

"Alex," she whimpered, "I'm scared!"

You're not the only one, Alex thought, but didn't say so.

"We've got to tell someone," said Devi.

Mags made a snorting noise and Alex

said, "Fine. Who'd believe us?"

"Mr Lawless might," Devi suggested.

They thought about that for a minute or two. Of all the people they could talk to, Mr Lawless was certainly the only one who might possibly take them seriously. But it was still a very slim hope.

Yet they had to do *something*. With a week to go before the panto performance, there was scope for the animals to cause a lot more mayhem – and what they might do at the performance itself didn't bear thinking about.

"If only Mr Lawless could see it for himself," Alex mused. "That would convince him."

"Not much chance of that," Mags said gloomily. "Haven't you noticed? There's never any real trouble when adults are around. Those creatures are very careful – they make sure that we're the only targets."

"Then maybe we could do something to force them into the open," Devi suggested. "I don't know: get them angry, perhaps, so that they show themselves when someone else is around."

"It's a thought." Alex looked interested. "But how could we do it?"

Mags shuddered. "It's all right for you two, but you've forgotten one thing: I've got to *wear* most of those animals as part of my costume. So if we get them angry, what's going to happen to me?"

"Mags, you can't!" Caroly said in alarm. "If that fox attacked you the way it did me—"

"All right, all right!" Alex waved her hands for peace. "Calm down, Caroly! Of course we're not going to put Mags in danger." She sighed. "Look, it's Saturday tomorrow, so we'll be at the school hall—"

"Not me!" Caroly interrupted. "I'm not going!"

"You don't have to; Mr Lawless would probably string you up from the curtain rail if you turned up. What I'm saying is, we'll be there all day, and so will Mr Lawless. I think there's a good chance something weird will happen. And when it does—"

"*If* it does," said Mags.

"*When*," Alex repeated firmly. "Then we talk to Mr Lawless. Agreed?"

"Well, it's not much of a hope," said Devi, "but it's the only one we've got."

Mags and Devi went home soon afterwards, and Alex and Caroly both had an early night. Lying in bed, Alex thought about the happenings of the past few days, and was plagued by sudden doubts. Was it *really* possible that they were being haunted – if haunted was the right word – by a bunch of spooky animals? Those creatures had all been dead for years and years. How could they have come to life again? Maybe their whole crazy theory was wrong. Maybe it really was the eco-warriors, and at this very moment Caroly was lying in bed sniggering. At least that was a rational explanation, whereas ghosts – or something even stranger – didn't make any sense at all.

She went to sleep with her mind still churning, and slept (though with some peculiar dreams) until three o'clock. Then something woke her.

She raised her head from the pillow. There was a noise on the landing outside. Something shuffling. . . Fear leaped, and Alex put a clenched fist over her mouth as her heart began to pound. Slowly, she reached towards the bedside lamp. . .

And jolted upright as though she'd had an electric shock, as her door flew open and a dark shape came crashing into the room.

"*Alex!*"

The scream on Alex's lips died as she heard Caroly's frantic wail, and her sister flung herself across the room and on to the bed. "Alex, help me! There's something trying to get in at my window!"

"Caroly, quiet! Shh!" Alex hugged her – she didn't have much choice, as Caroly was clinging on with all her strength. "You'll wake Mum and Dad! What's going on?"

"S-something outside my *window*," Caroly repeated, more quietly now, but snivelling. "I heard it! Oh Alex—"

"It was probably a nightmare," Alex soothed.

"It wasn't! It isn't! Oh Alex, *do* something!"

"Calm down!" Alex managed to extricate herself from Caroly's grasp and got out of bed. "Come on. We'll both go and see."

She took her torch and, with Caroly shivering behind her, went to the next-door bedroom. Closing the door, she listened. There was no sound.

Then. . .

Scri-i-itch. . . It came from the direction of the window. Outside.

"It's probably the Virginia creeper on the wall," Alex whispered. But suddenly she wasn't so sure.

Scri-itch. Tap-tap-tap.

That was *not* the Virginia creeper, Alex thought.

It sounded like claws on the glass.

Or a bird's talons. . .

In a single moment all Alex's earlier doubts vanished. She started to tiptoe across the room.

"Alex, be careful!" Caroly whimpered.

Alex ignored her. *How stupid can I get?* she thought. *Chaz did this, and Mags and I tried to warn him, and look what happened!*

She forced the thought of Chaz away. Her thumb was on the torch switch and her hand was shaking, but she tried not to notice. Three more steps to the window; two; one. . . Taking a deep breath, Alex reached out with her other hand and wrenched the curtain back.

There was a scuffle and a flurry, and a big silhouette launched itself away from the window-pane and flapped off into the night. Alex leaped back, crashing into Caroly, and they retreated to the far side of the room.

"Wh-what was it?" Caroly whispered.

"I don't know." *But I can guess,* Alex thought. *That owl. Yet again.*

Suddenly she felt a surge of anger at the creatures, and to Caroly's horror she strode back to the window and flung it open. Switching the torch on, she stabbed the beam into the darkness, casting it in a wide circle across the back garden.

There was a commotion in Dad's hydrangeas, and four shadows, of different shapes and sizes, bolted away across the snow-covered lawn and vanished in the night.

"I saw you!" Alex hissed furiously. Four of them, huh? She didn't know what they were, but she'd take a guess that one was a fox. Sweeping the torch again she saw that the whole lawn was criss-crossed with little footprints, just as the school grounds had been on Thursday morning. What *were* these creatures? Were they ghosts, or were they, somehow, real and physical?

Then the question that no one had yet thought to ask dropped abruptly into her mind.

"Why are you doing this?" She whispered the words out into the night. "What do you *want*?"

Nothing responded. The garden was still and silent again. Alex drew back into the bedroom, shut the window and switched the torch off. She was frowning.

"What did you see?" Caroly said nervously.

"There's nothing out there. Not any more."

"I heard you whispering." Caroly sounded almost accusing.

"I was just muttering to myself. Look, you can

go back to bed now. There isn't going to be any more trouble tonight."

"I want my light on!"

"Well, have it, then. But whatever it was, it isn't going to come back."

Caroly looked dubious. "Promise?"

"Promise." Alex was certain, though she didn't quite know why. She had had no answer to her question, but she had a funny feeling that it had been heard, and that the creatures were thinking about it.

Or was that idea just totally crazy?

She pushed the thought away. *Wait till tomorrow,* she told herself. *See what happens then.*

Because something was going to. She was absolutely sure of that.

11

Alex, Mags and Devi were at the school hall by a quarter to nine the next morning. It was snowing again, and there was no one in sight, but Mr Lawless's car was parked outside and a single trail of footprints led through the fresh snow to the door.

Mr Lawless was on the stage – and the moment they saw him, they knew something was wrong.

"Ah." He turned as they came in, and his brows knitted together in a menacing frown. "Alex. Just the person I want to see!"

"What's up, Mr L?" Alex asked.

"Come up here." Mr Lawless beckoned.

"All of you."

They exchanged uneasy glances and climbed on to the platform. Mr Lawless led them backstage to where the scenery flats were, and pointed at the stacked woodland scenes which he and Alex had so carefully painted the previous weekend.

The smooth edges along the bottoms of the flats weren't smooth any more. They were split and ragged. In places, whole chunks had been taken out of them. And up to a height of about half a metre, the paint was scraped and scratched and ruined.

Alex said: "What on earth—?"

"Oh, come on, Alex!" Mr Lawless interrupted. "I know Caroly's your sister, but loyalty's got limits! This is downright sabotage, and it's gone too far!"

Mags was still staring at the damaged scenery. "Those edges look as if they've been *chewed*. . ." she said.

"Ten out of ten, Mags – they have!" Mr Lawless told her. "Do you know what I found behind the stack? Rabbit droppings! And for good measure, there's bird lime all over the back of the flats, as if a whole flock of sparrows has been roosting on them!" He glared at Alex.

"Your sister and her little friends have really pulled the stops out this time! When I get my hands on them—"

"Mr Lawless—" said Alex.

He wasn't listening. "I don't know how the heck they did it, but it must have taken some planning, and—"

"No, Mr Lawless, you don't understand—"

"—got all this mess from the park, I suppose—"

"Mr *Lawless*! They didn't do it – it really *was* animals!"

"And what with that and the other stuff that's suddenly gone missing—"

"What?"

"What?"

The two "whats" came out as a chorus, as Mr Lawless and Alex both took in what the other had said. Then: "Missing?" repeated Alex, and "What do you mean, it really was animals?" demanded Mr Lawless.

There was a short silence. Alex, Mags and Devi looked unhappily at each other. Finally, it was Devi who spoke.

"Mr Lawless, what's gone missing?" she asked in a small voice.

Mr Lawless sighed exasperatedly. "More

scenery. Half those crêpe-paper leaves that Year Eight spent so much time and effort making have gone. There's just the bare twigs left, as if they've been eaten!"

Alex bit her lip. "They probably have."

Mr Lawless snorted. "By rabbits, I suppose!"

"Sort of. But . . . not exactly."

"Right." Mr Lawless stood up straight and gave them all a look that could have melted metal. "Before the others get here, I think you'd better tell me *exactly* what's going on!"

He didn't want to believe it, of course. He wanted to rant furiously that the whole thing was completely mad, and they must think he was brainless if he'd fall for such a ludicrous tale. But two things stopped him.

The first was that there simply wasn't a rational explanation for what had happened. As Alex argued, how could Caroly's mates have got in, done the damage and got out again? The school was locked up at night, they hadn't got keys, and there was no sign of any break-in. Mr Lawless had to admit that he didn't have an answer to that mystery.

And the second thing was Devi. Unlike Alex and Mags, Devi was far too sensible to let her imagination run riot: more to the point, she wasn't the kind of person to get involved in silly tricks. The business about the crocodile footprints – Devi didn't tell lies or play games. She meant it. She believed this story. And that gave Mr Lawless a very uncomfortable feeling.

"All right," he said at last, when they had finished. "I'm not going to say that this tale could possibly be true. But . . . I'm not going to say that it couldn't, either."

The three breathed huge sighs of relief.

"What we *have* got to do," Mr Lawless continued, "is prove it, one way or the other."

"That's what we thought," Mags agreed. "Only we don't know how."

"Well," said Mr Lawless, "what I suggest is—"

The door at the end of the hall banged at that moment, interrupting him, and they looked up to see Robbie Blake and a group of other helpers and friends coming in.

"Sorry we're late, Mr Lawless, the bus took years," said Robbie. "There's some more people coming up the drive. Did you know it's snowing again?"

Alex muttered something under her breath, and Mr Lawless said quietly, "I'll talk to you three later. For now, let's just get down to work."

There were no horrible happenings during the morning. The hall rang to the sounds of hammering, sawing and Mr Lawless's electric drill, and the noise increased as the helpers who were also in the cast practised their lines out loud. Alex and Robbie re-painted the damaged scenery, dazzled now and then by colourful flashes as the stage lights were tested. Then three people started complaining that their costumes didn't fit properly, and Alex spent the next hour up to her ears in material, pins and Sellotape as she made hasty alterations. Hours flew by, and before any of them knew it, it was time to break for lunch.

Alex, Mags and Devi took their sandwiches and found a quiet corner well away from everyone else. Alex was worried.

"I don't like it," she said. "We get here to find there's been mayhem in the night, then all morning nothing happens. They've gone too quiet."

Devi agreed. "It's as if they know we want to prove our story to Mr Lawless, and they're deliberately lying low." She shivered. "That's creepy. Like they can read our minds."

Alex remembered the question she had asked last night, whispering it into the dark as she leaned out of Caroly's bedroom window. She felt sure that the animals *did* want something, but if the sabotage in the hall this morning was a clue, she didn't understand what it meant.

"We're going to rehearse some of the main scenes this afternoon," Mags reminded them. "They might do something then."

"Yes," said Devi uneasily. "They might. Don't wear your costume, Mags!"

Mags shook her head. "I think I've got to. I know what we said last night, but if it tempts them to start any trouble . . . well, that's what we want, isn't it?" She forced a grin. "Besides, you know me. Anything for a laugh."

As they were all finishing their lunches, Imogen Lawless arrived, wearing a moth-eaten Afghan coat over the usual floaty dress, and with snow in her hair. She came into the hall staggering under the bulk of several enormous packages, and dropped the lot in the middle of the floor among the pile of clutter already there.

"Trees!" she announced triumphantly, and crossed the floor to give Mr Lawless a smacking kiss, to a chorus of hoots and whistles. Mr Lawless made a rude gesture to the whistlers and told them to get the packages up on to the stage.

Imogen had made four wonderful papier-mâché trees for the pantomime wood. They fitted together in sections, and were to be placed towards the front of the stage to make the scenery more three-dimensional. Even without leaves (at least until the Year Eights could make some more) they looked very convincing, and Mr Lawless said that they might as well rehearse the wood scenes first, and get used to having the trees in position.

The cast scrambled to get ready, while Mr Lawless sorted out the music tapes. Mags wasn't in this part of the show and so her costume wasn't needed, but as Alex helped Patsy and Sean, the two halves of the pantomime horse, to get ready, she kept a wary eye on the props box, half expecting to see the lid creak open and something furry or slinky creep out. Nothing did. But by the time they were ready to begin, she was feeling distinctly jittery.

The jitters faded a little as the rehearsal got under way and everything went smoothly. No one forgot their lines, no one collided with anyone else, and Imogen, who hadn't seen this part of the pantomime before, laughed uproariously in all the right places. Devi had another comic dance to perform, this time with the Seven Dwarfs and the panto horse, and as their music blared out Mags came to stand beside Alex.

"I love this bit," she whispered as the dance began. "Devi's great, isn't she? I don't know how she keeps her face so straight!"

Alex opened her mouth to reply. But though her mouth stayed open, no sound came out.

"Alex?" Mags elbowed her. "I said. . ." Then she stopped as she saw Alex's expression.

Alex was staring fixedly at the stage. At one of the papier-mâché trees.

"What—" Mags began.

She didn't finish, because Alex grabbed her arm in a painful grip and hissed, "*Shh! Watch!*"

Baffled, Mags watched. The panto horse was cavorting around the stage, while the Dwarfs scurried and ducked and hid among the four trees, popping their heads out and pulling faces. It was one of the funniest moments in the show. But Alex wasn't laughing.

Then, as a dwarf jumped out from behind a tree, Mags saw it. On the other side of the trunk, something else appeared. A face. A very small, sharp, furry face. It peeked out, then dived out of sight again.

It was a fox.

"Alex. . ." Mags said quaveringly.

"I know." Alex's voice was grim. Then they both jumped violently as another face showed itself and vanished again.

"*That was a badger!*" Mags gasped. "But we haven't got any badger bits . . . have we?"

Alex was shivering. "What about all the fur trimmings on your hat and gloves? We've never asked ourselves what they are; we just – *ah*!"

It was a bird this time. It looked horribly like a parrot, and Alex remembered all the feathers on Horrida's hat. The feathers that kept coming off and scattering themselves all over the place. . .

Then, up in the tree's curling branches, she saw something else. Something very long and thin, that slithered with a malevolent, sinuous movement.

"Oh, no. . ." she whispered. "It can't be – it *can't*!"

The slithering thing slipped out of sight behind the tree. Alex was paralysed. She didn't know what to do, but alarm was starting to turn into cold terror. *If that was what she thought it was—*

Suddenly Mags grabbed her again. "Alex, look at Imogen!"

Alex's head flicked round. Imogen Lawless was also staring up at the tree. She had stopped laughing. Instead, her face bore a look of astonished horror.

"She saw it, too!" gasped Mags.

They started to hurry towards Imogen, whose face had now turned pale. But before they could reach her, there was a commotion on stage. The panto horse, which had been dancing round the fateful tree, suddenly leaped into the air, twisting and turning, its legs kicking wildly. And from inside the costume came a shriek:

"*Aagh! Get it off me! GET IT OFF!*"

12

"*It's a snake! It's a snake! Aagh, HELP!!*"

Both halves of the panto horse were screaming at the tops of their voices, and thrashing around so much that no one could get near them. Only when Mr Lawless and Robbie Blake sat on them were they at last able to get the costume unzipped.

Patsy rolled out on to the stage, still yelling, and Sean's flailing arm whacked Robbie in the face as he struggled after her. Grabbing the costume, Mr Lawless shook it fiercely.

One of Horrida's gloves fell out.

"There's your snake!" Robbie pointed at it, then creased up with laughter.

Sean and Patsy stared. "But. . ." Patsy began.

"I thought. . ." Sean swallowed. "It was *moving*!"

"Course it was, with you two clomping around in there," said Robbie, sitting back on his heels. "Hey, that was brilliant! Shall we keep it in the show, Mr L?"

Mr Lawless didn't answer. He was frowning. When Alex and Mags looked at Imogen, they saw that her face was absolutely dead white now. And Devi was standing very, very still, with her eyes shut and one hand clamped over her mouth.

Alex started to say breathlessly, "Mr Lawless, did you. . ."

The words died as Mr Lawless shot her a warning glance that told her to shut up.

"OK, you lot," he said with a pretence of cheerfulness that didn't fool Alex and Mags. "Panic over. Patsy, Sean, sit this out for a while, until you've recovered from the scare. We'll run through the soppy love scene with Prince Twit instead. Oh, and someone retrieve that glove and put it back in the cupboard, please."

"He doesn't want to touch it," Mags whispered to Alex.

"He's not the only one!" Alex replied fervently. "Robbie's doing it. Look."

They watched apprehensively as Robbie unsuspectingly picked up the glove and walked off with it. But there were no more screams, and he came back safely a minute later.

The rehearsal got going again. Devi was very shaky to begin with, stammering her lines and missing several cues, but after a while things settled down. The faces in the trees didn't appear again. But once or twice Alex heard what sounded like fluttering noises, high above her head among the tangle of lights and wires and curtain tracks. She looked up nervously, but there was nothing there.

At least, nothing visible.

By the time they finished, at four o'clock, there had been no more trouble. Mr Lawless said that there was no need to worry about clearing up; he already had a few volunteers to help, and they'd all be back again tomorrow anyway. Everyone was delighted to be let off lightly, and within minutes only five people were left in the hall.

The "volunteers", of course, were Alex, Mags and Devi. The fifth person was Imogen. She and Mr Lawless had had a quiet but urgent discussion during the rehearsal. The girls didn't know how much he had told her, but it was clear from the look on her face that she knew at least the bones of the story.

They gathered together on the stage. For a few moments no one said anything, then Alex spoke up.

"Did you see it, Mr Lawless? In the tree?"

Mr Lawless looked uneasy. "I saw something. And I know it *looked* like a snake. But—"

"It was!" Mags insisted. "And the other creatures—"

"I didn't see them."

"But I did," said Imogen. "I told him."

"Mr Lawless, you've got to believe us now!" Alex pleaded.

Mr Lawless sighed. "I don't know. The whole idea's so incredible! If we can find some logical explanation—"

The three girls all burst out in protest at once.

"It *is* true!"

"There isn't a logical explanation!"

"Mr *Lawless*!"

"All right, all right!" He held up both hands for peace. "I only said *if* we can find a logical explanation. And I've got a suggestion. In fact, it was Imogen's idea."

Imogen nodded. "I'll tell you about it, but not here. Anyone got a lift waiting? No? Good. Then let's all go to our car."

They finished packing up, then all five of them hurried through the snow to the Lawlesses' red Volkswagen. When they were all inside, Imogen explained.

The idea was simple. Whoever or whatever was behind this trouble, most of their mischief took place after everyone had gone home and the school was deserted. Imogen proposed that they should pretend to leave, drive round the block a couple of times, then sneak back and set up a watch, to see if they could catch the troublemakers at work.

Alex and Mags were enthusiastic. Devi was more wary, but there was no way she was going to be left out. Imogen said there was no time like the present, so how about doing it tonight?

"Hold on, Imogen," said Mr Lawless. "We're rushing things a bit."

"No, we're not," Imogen countered. "This thing's getting out of hand; you said so yourself. So the sooner we get to the bottom of it, the safer your panto – and everyone in it – will be."

Mr Lawless was outnumbered and he knew it. "OK," he said, "I give in." He glanced at the girls in the back seat. "But if any of you think for one minute that your parents would object—"

"They wouldn't, Mr Lawless," said Alex firmly. "Not if we're with you and Imogen."

Mr Lawless said something under his breath, and Imogen laughed as she started the car.

They drove around town for half an hour, then headed back towards the school. As they went down one particular road, Mags suddenly murmured to Alex,

"This is Chaz Peterson's street, isn't it?"

She was right. "Which house is his?" Alex muttered back.

"I'm not sure; I think it's that one with the – *oh, stop the car*!"

Imogen slammed on the brakes and almost skidded, and Mr Lawless exclaimed, "Whatever's the matter?"

"Look!" Mags pointed through the window. "By Chaz's gate – in the snow."

They all peered, and Alex felt an awful lurching in the pit of her stomach.

There were footprints in the fresh snow outside the gate of Chaz's house. They crisscrossed in all directions, going backwards, forwards and round in circles, as though the feet that made them had been scuffing and pacing impatiently up and down outside.

And they weren't human feet.

Devi whispered: "*The crocodile. . .*"

There was a long, horrible silence. Then:

"I can't see any lights on in the house," said Imogen uneasily.

"What's going on?" Alex's voice shook. "What's happened to Chaz?"

Suddenly Mr Lawless opened the car door and got out. They called after him to be careful, but he took no notice. He pushed the gate open and strode up the path. A light did come on when he rang the bell, and a few moments later Chaz's mum opened the door. The others saw the two of them talking but couldn't hear what was said. Then the door closed, and Mr Lawless turned to come back to the car.

He reached the gate again – and stopped. There was a high privet hedge at the front of the garden, lit now by the car headlights. In the hedge, something was moving. They couldn't actually see it, but they could see the hedge shaking as its leaves were disturbed.

"It's all right," said Imogen. "It's only a cat or something." But her voice was quavering, and her knuckles had turned white on the steering wheel.

The shaking in the hedge stopped. Mr Lawless took a step towards the road.

The shaking began again, moving towards him.

"Andy. . ." There was terror in Imogen's voice now. "Andy, come back! Get in the car, *quickly*!"

The shaking increased with a violence that dislodged a small avalanche of snow from the top of the hedge. Near panic, Imogen revved the car so hard that clouds of smoke came out of the exhaust pipe and the roar of the engine echoed down the street. The entire hedge seemed to quiver from end to end.

And suddenly everything was absolutely still.

But only for a moment. Mr Lawless didn't hang about to see if anything else would happen; he was through the gate in a single stride and running back to the car. As he slammed the door, Imogen accelerated away down the road, and only stopped again when they were well clear of the house.

Four pairs of eyes fixed on Mr Lawless. "What did you see?" Imogen demanded.

"I didn't *see* anything," said Mr Lawless

tensely, "but I heard it. And no animal I've ever encountered makes a noise like that!"

"What about Chaz?" Alex asked breathlessly. "Is he all right?"

"Oh, Chaz is fine, his mum says. I just pretended I was calling to ask after him and tell him not to worry about the panto. She told me that he pulled out because he's been having bad dreams about it."

Silence. Devi shuddered and huddled more deeply into her coat.

"I think," said Mr Lawless grimly, "that it's about time we went back to the hall." He paused. "Though anyone who doesn't want to now can say so, and we'll take you home."

Alex thought quickly. She *was* scared, but if she gave up now, what would happen? Things weren't going to get any better. Unless something was done, and quickly, they could only get worse.

She glanced at Mags and Devi, who both nodded. "No," she said, hoping she sounded more confident than she felt. "We'll all come. We've got to, haven't we?"

The car pulled away again, making for the school. When it had gone, the street was quiet. There was no more traffic, nothing to be seen but the tyre tracks. The falling snow quickly began to cover them, as it had covered the tracks and prints of earlier passing cars, and after a few minutes the roadway looked smoothly white again.

Except for one thing.

A single trail of prints. Not human. Crossing the road from the Petersons' gate, and following a perfectly straight line that took no account of buildings or any other obstacle.

Leading directly towards the school grounds.

13

The school and its surroundings were dark and deserted. They parked the car out of sight of the hall, and to avoid triggering the security light Mr Lawless led them in through the caretaker's door. The door didn't fit very well; it was a bit of a struggle to get it open and shut again, but at last he managed, and switched on the pocket torch from the car's glove compartment.

A small beam lit up the narrow passage ahead.

"There's a bigger torch in the caretaker's cupboard," Mr Lawless said, speaking very quietly. "We'll take that, too."

"C-couldn't we put a light on?" asked Devi hopefully. "Just one?"

"Better not. We don't want to give away the fact that we're here." There were rummaging noises as Mr Lawless searched in the cupboard, then a second and much stronger torch beam came on. "That's better." He handed the little torch to Imogen. "Right. Come on."

This was no longer the everyday, familiar school that Alex knew so well. It was suddenly a place of menace, with strangeness in every corner and shadows lurking and shifting at the edges of the torch beams. Once she thought she heard a sound behind them, but when they all paused and listened there was nothing.

But as they approached the hall, their ears picked up a noise. It was very faint, like a murmuring and a grunting and a rustling – and it was coming from the other side of the hall doors.

Mr Lawless stopped, and switched off his torch. Alex heard Devi gasp as they were plunged into darkness, and reached out to grip her hand reassuringly.

"Don't be scared!" she whispered.

"Shh!" said Mr Lawless. "Listen."

They could hear the noises from inside the

hall more clearly now. Rustling. Shuffling. Pattering. Very *busy* sounds. And the murmuring . . . though it wasn't exactly a murmur, more of a twitter. Like birds, or small animals. Straining her ears, Alex tried to judge whether any of the noises suggested something bigger, but she couldn't be sure.

Their eyes had adjusted to the dark enough for them to see Mr Lawless beckoning them back from the door.

"All right," he said softly. "There's someone – or something – in there; no doubt of it. We'll go in from behind the stage, and try to get close enough for a look. Better not use the torches. Can you manage without them?"

The others nodded and moved off quietly, retracing their steps to the main corridor. Alex, near the back of the group, kept her gaze firmly fixed on the dim, tall shape of Mr Lawless in the lead. With no bobbing circle of torchlight the shadows were worse than unnerving, and an unpleasant prickling sensation kept crawling over the back of her neck and down her spine.

Then, from behind her, came a stifled cry.

Alex jumped violently and swung round. The cry had come from Devi. She was pressed against the wall, shoulders hunched in terror and both hands clapped to her mouth as if to stop herself from screaming. Through her fingers her voice came muffled and quaking:

"*Something touched me!*"

Alex froze, her stomach lurching horribly. Then a pencil of light stabbed into the darkness and Imogen was there with her torch.

"Devi, it's all right. There's nothing there." She scanned the beam around, showing only the bare floor. But Devi couldn't be convinced.

"There *was* something," she insisted. "I felt it. It touched my leg." She was shaking like a jelly and almost in tears. "I can't do this! I want to go back!"

"Come on, Dev," Alex coaxed. "We're all together. Nothing's going to hurt you!"

Devi shook her head. "No! I can't. I'm sorry. . ."

"All right," said Imogen. "I think it's best if Devi goes back to the car. Alex, will you go with her? Here, take my torch."

Alex put an arm round Devi's shoulders and shepherded her away. As they headed for the side door, Devi kept apologizing for her cowardice.

"It's all right," Alex said. "Tell you the truth, I was getting scared, too. It's all very well being brave in theory, but it's totally different when you're actually facing it."

Devi managed a little laugh. "I thought it was just me."

"Well, it isn't. Come on. As they say in the movies, let's get outa here!"

They turned into the passage that led to the caretaker's door. Then, three steps into it, Alex stopped dead.

She was shining the torch along the floor ahead of them. And the beam had shown up something lying in their path.

Devi said in a small, frightened voice: "Oh, no. . ."

It was the handbag. It was lying on its side with the clasp towards them, and it was wide open. For a hideous moment the thought jangled through Alex's imagination that the dark interior looked exactly like a mouth.

Devi whispered: "How. . .?" but didn't finish the question. There was no need to.

"It's only a handbag," said Alex slowly. "A thing. An object. It isn't alive."

"Neither's the owl. . ." There was an awful tremor in Devi's voice.

"*No!*" Alex gripped her arm, shaking it. "Don't think like that. It can't possibly hurt us.

All I've got to do is pick it up."

"Alex, *don't*!"

But Alex took no notice. She moved towards the handbag, bent down, reached out.

The bag didn't do anything. As she had said, it was only an object. Her fingers closed round the strap and she lifted it up. It certainly was heavy. Much heavier than she remembered, in fact; as if there were stones or something in it. Alex leaned to peer into its depths, pointing the torch. . .

The bag twisted in her hand, wrenching itself out of her grasp. It *leaped* at her – and the clasp snapped, like an attacking predator, at her face.

Alex shrieked. Her hand flailed, swatting the bag away. She heard Devi scream, too; saw the bag spinning through the air to land with a skidding thud somewhere in the dark ahead of them. Then panic overtook everything else, and in an instant they were scrambling and stumbling out of the passage, back into the main corridor where, gasping and trembling, they collapsed against the far wall.

Devi was crying, in huge, gulping sobs of sheer terror, and Alex pressed her face to the cold wall, trying to recover from the shock and get herself under control. The lunging jaws of the handbag had missed her face by a hair's breadth. If they hadn't missed, what would have happened? Would the bag have turned into a real animal – the animal it had once been?

Then, from the deep darkness of the passage, she heard a noise.

It was a slithering, slapping noise, like the sound of a heavy bulk moving slowly. And it was coming towards them.

Devi heard it too. Her sobbing stopped and she stood paralysed, staring at the passage entrance as the noise came inexorably closer and closer. Part of Alex's mind screamed that this wasn't happening – but another part, far more powerful, yelled a silent, blazing command to *run*!

"Devi, move!" she urged through clamped teeth. "Move, now!"

"I c-c-can't!" Devi whimpered.

"You can! Run, Devi, *run*!" Frantically Alex grabbed Devi's arm and dug her fingernails as hard as she could into the flesh. Devi yelped – then her paralysis snapped and together they pounded away along the corridor.

They didn't know where they were going and didn't care; all that mattered was to get away.

Alex wielded the torch like a weapon, the beam swinging wildly from side to side to ward off anything that might try to stop them. *I can't hear it following; oh, please God don't let it be following*! Pushing the terrified Devi before her she raced on, until the swaying torchlight showed a glass-panelled door directly ahead.

"It's the door by the staff room! Come *on*!" Putting on a spurt, Alex flung herself at the door and scrabbled with the handle.

The handle – it wasn't turning. It wouldn't work!

"Oh, no! They're all locked, of course they are!"

"What are we going to *do*?" Devi wailed.

"Wait a minute; wait, wait." Alex held her breath, listening. But the thing she dreaded – the slithering, slapping sound of the moving horror – had stopped. It wasn't coming after them. It had given up the chase.

At least for the moment. . .

"Mr Lawless has got the keys," she said. "We'll have to go back to the hall."

"I'm not going anywhere near that passage!"

"Neither am I. But there's another way round, past the Head's office."

"Can't we break the glass instead?" Devi pleaded.

"No. For one thing, we probably wouldn't be strong enough. And for another, we've got to warn the others!"

Devi hadn't thought of that, and her eyes widened. "If it crept up on them—"

"Exactly. Come on. Quickly, and quietly."

It seemed to take a nightmare age to reach the hall by the longer route. Each moment was an agony of strain and suspicion that set the blood pounding thickly in their veins and stretched every nerve to breaking point. But nothing leaped at them out of the darkness. They heard no eerie sounds. And at last they reached the short flight of stairs that led to the hall's backstage entrance.

Alex approached the door first.

And stopped.

"I can't hear anything," she whispered to Devi. "Nothing at all."

"Why should you?" Devi whispered back. "They're probably hiding. Waiting for something to happen." She stifled a hysterical giggle.

"I know, but. . ." Alex couldn't explain the feeling that was crawling inside her. It was pure instinct and she didn't have any grounds for it, but this felt *wrong*.

She eased the door open a crack and peered through. No movement in the gloom . . . but there *was* a slight noise now. A whispering. Human voices? Alex thought so but couldn't be absolutely sure.

"Wait here," she said in Devi's ear. "I'm going to take a closer look."

She slid round the door and tiptoed forward. Immediately there was a peculiar fluttering sound above her head, as if something up among the curtain mechanism and lighting rails had seen her and scurried away. Alex shivered. But at least whatever moved had sounded small. . .

Warily, she shone the torch into the area. There was the familiar backstage clutter. The stacked scenery. Two trestle tables. The props box. . .

Alex swung the torch back to focus on the props box again. It was *open*.

But she had seen Mr Lawless lock it, the way he always did when they packed up.

Heart leaping, Alex crept forward. She meant to look in the props box, to see if anything was missing. But before she could reach it someone whimpered on the other side of the stage backdrop.

And a low voice, that she recognized instantly as Mr Lawless's, said:

"No, Mags! Keep still – just keep still!"

A sensation of icy dread spread from the pit of Alex's stomach. Shielding the torch beam with her fingers, she moved stealthily towards the backdrop. There was a gap at the edge. If she could just reach it without falling over anything. . .

She did, and pressed her face to the gap. A glimmer of light showed on the far side of the stage, and she realized that it was Mr Lawless's torch. But it wasn't moving. Shaking, yes, but not moving. What was happening out there?

Alex peeped through the gap.

Mr Lawless, Imogen and Mags were huddled together on the far side of the stage. Alex could only see their silhouettes, but they were clearly cornered – and terrified.

Then her heart seemed to turn over inside her as, by the glow of Mr Lawless's unsteady torch, she saw what had gathered on the stage boards.

Animals. A throng of animals. Rabbits and birds, badgers and stoats. A fox. A stag. An owl. Two snakes, their heads raised, their bodies coiled. All motionless, all staring at the three frightened humans. *Glaring* at them. The birds' beaks were threateningly open. And the other creatures bared teeth in silent, menacing snarls.

And, in their midst so that they were ranged around and behind it, was something else.

A handbag. . .

14

"You know what you've got to do?" By the torch's tiny light Alex watched Devi's scared face, hoping and praying that the other girl's nerve would hold.

Devi nodded. "When you signal, throw this switch."

"Right. And the signal's three flashes of the torch." It was a wild idea, but Alex thought it could work. Surprise – that was the key. Catch them off guard.

She looked up at the tangle of wires and struts and fabric overhead – all the chaos of the hall's technical end. It wasn't actually very high up, and her head for heights was OK. She just prayed that there wasn't anything else up there, waiting for her.

She heard Devi wince as she started to move away, and whispered back, "Don't be scared. They won't come back here; they're only interested in Mags and the others."

"I kn-know," came Devi's quavering reply. "But it's so d-d-dark without the torch."

Dark enough even with it, Alex thought. And once she got up among the tangle, she'd have to switch it off or risk giving herself away to the creatures below. Maybe this was a deeply stupid idea after all.

Shut up! her inner self said savagely. *Stupid or not, you can't think of anything better. So get on with it!*

The helpers who worked the spotlights used a tall stepladder to reach their perches above the stage, and by sheer good luck it hadn't been put away. Alex climbed up carefully, holding her breath at each nerve-racking wobble, and in less than a minute her hands were on the nearest lighting bar.

There was just one spotlight here, but it was a big one, and its angle could be adjusted by a knurled knob. Alex turned the knob (*don't squeak or grate, please don't!*) and looked down through the struts and wires to where Mr Lawless's torch lit the eerie scene beneath.

The animals hadn't moved. It was as if they were waiting for something to happen. From here, Alex could see Mags, Imogen and Mr Lawless more clearly. They, too, were motionless, afraid to do anything that might provoke the creatures to attack. The knob freed at last, and very gingerly Alex started to alter the angle of the spotlight.

Then, a metre from where she crouched, something moved.

Shock slammed through Alex and almost pitched her off the ladder. She grabbed for a handhold, found one and steadied herself. *Idiot!* It was just a cable, disturbed by the movement of the light. It tapped against the bar, gently, then settled.

And Mr Lawless's eyes swivelled upwards.

He saw her, and she saw his eyes widen. She put a finger to her mouth, quickly, urgently, warning him not to react, and to her relief he looked away again.

A few more centimetres and the spotlight would be in position, or as good a position as she could guess at. Alex twisted the knob again, securing it. Then she turned round, and flashed the torch three times.

What happened next was so sudden and so startling that, even though she knew what to expect, Alex could hardly take it in. Devi hit the switch and the spotlight leaped to life, flooding the stage with a glare of green brilliance. Mags and Imogen both yelled aloud in shock – and the legion of creatures seemed to explode outwards like a bomb blast. Alex had a stunning, momentary impression of a small tide of shapes hurtling in all directions, fleeing from the light and vanishing like smoke on a wind. Then suddenly there was noise and chaos, as Mr Lawless ran forward, shielding his eyes from the glare and calling her name, while Mags and Imogen stumbled across the stage and Devi came rushing to join them.

Somehow, Alex got down the ladder and they all collided together on the stage. Everyone was babbling their own story and at first no one could make any sense of anything. But eventually some calm was restored.

Mr Lawless's group had crept into the hall by the side door in time to hear the scuttering and scuffling of many feet scampering away. They'd ventured on to the stage and in the torchlight they had seen all the animal props strewn on the boards, with Horrida's handbag in the middle. Remembering Chaz (and they hadn't known, then, what had happened to Alex and Devi), no one had wanted to go near the bag. But eventually Mr Lawless had started to approach.

Before he could reach it, the props had vanished and the animals had appeared in their place. They had surrounded him, then silently drove him back to where Mags and Imogen were cowering. When they were cornered, the animals had simply stopped, and stared at them.

"It was as if they were trying to say something," said Mr Lawless solemnly. "But we couldn't understand."

Alex remembered what had happened when *something* tried to get into Caroly's bedroom. The question she had asked. . .

"They *are* trying to talk to us," she said. "I'm sure of it. They want something."

"Revenge?" suggested Mags nervously. "On the people who killed them?"

"Maybe," said Imogen. "But *we* didn't kill them. They all died years ago!"

"Perhaps that doesn't make any difference," said Mr Lawless. "We're human. Perhaps that's enough."

But Alex didn't think so. They were still standing in the glare of the spotlight, and now she looked around at the stage boards.

The props were all there: the stag's head, the stuffed owl, the gloves, the fox fur, the hat with its feathers scattered all over the place again. She couldn't begin to understand how any of this was possible, but something was nagging at the back of her brain.

Suddenly, on impulse, she snatched up the fox-fur wrap and held it so that the head was only centimetres from her nose. The glass eyes stared blankly at her and the fur didn't come to life.

But she knew with absolute certainty that the fox – or its spirit – could hear her.

"Show us!" she said aloud, gripping the fur tightly and shaking it. "Just show us what it is you want!"

The others looked at her as if she'd gone crazy. But Alex saw something that they didn't. For a moment, just one, the fox's glass eyes gleamed with an inner light. A pulse went through Alex's hands, as if the fur had breathed.

And from overhead came a soft, urgent twittering.

"The curtains!" Imogen's eyes widened.

"Look! Something's trying to move them!"

They all stared up at the rail where the curtains hung. It was hard to be sure, but Alex thought she had a glimpse of wings fluttering, and of several small shapes, like mice, scurrying along the rail. The curtains were too heavy for the creatures to move. They flapped and juddered, but they stayed in place.

"The winding mechanism!" said Alex breathlessly. "They want us to close the curtains!"

Mr Lawless ran to the side of the stage. He turned the handle that controlled the curtains, and slowly, slowly, they swished across the stage.

In the blaze of the spotlight, they all saw a word emblazoned in green paint across the curtains' entire width.

Just one word. But it said everything.

HOME.

"That's what they want. . ." Alex whispered. "A home. A place to live."

"But they're not alive," Mags breathed, wonderingly. "They're not real. They're. . ." She fumbled for the right word but couldn't find it.

Imogen smiled sadly. "Not real? Well, in one way I suppose not. But in another. . ." She gave an odd, nervous little laugh. "They're real enough to have shown themselves to us, aren't they? In all kinds of ways."

A soft chirruping came from overhead, as if something had heard and was agreeing with her.

"Poor little things," said Imogen. "All they want is peace."

"For their spirits?" asked Devi.

"Yes, I think so. Don't you?"

Devi's brow creased. "But what home can we give them? The costume cupboard? The props box? They're not exactly ideal, are they?"

"Wait a minute," said Alex. She had been thinking hard, and an idea was forming in her mind. It was bizarre – but then the animals were bizarre, too. Somehow, it all seemed to fit.

She started to say, "What if we—"

But she didn't get any further.

Because, on the stage, something had started to move.

15

They had all forgotten the handbag. It was still lying where they'd left it, surrounded by the other things. But as they looked at it in dawning alarm, the clasp began to yawn open, gaping widely. Like a mouth. Then the whole bag *writhed.*

A weird, murky mist started to appear around it. It grew, thickened . . . and began to form a shape. A long shape. Sinuous. Scaly. A tail that swept slowly, angrily from side to side. A huge, prehistoric head, its long jaw full of deadly teeth, its tiny eyes glittering with malevolence. Four squat, powerful legs, with clawed feet. . .

Devi made an awful choking sound. Mags

and Imogen clutched at each other. And Mr Lawless hissed, "*Get back! Get away from it!*"

He shoved them all behind him, pushing them towards the side of the stage, as the crocodile's head swung hungrily and its stare fixed on them.

"No. . ." Mags gasped. "Oh, please, someone *do* something!"

"It didn't appear with the others," Mr Lawless said grimly. "This one's got a mind of its own."

The thought slammed into Alex's head: *And it isn't like the others, either. It's a rebel, a loner, and it doesn't just want to give us a message. It wants more than that. It hates. It wants to kill. . .*

Then on the heels of that, and the panic it brought, came a surge of inspiration. She didn't pause – if she had, she would have lost her nerve – but dived out from behind Mr Lawless and sprinted across the stage.

"*Alex!*" Mr Lawless yelled.

Alex ignored him. She grabbed the first of the animal props she could find – it happened to be the stuffed owl – and held it up.

"Help us!" she cried. "Drive it away! Help us, *please*!"

Not a feather stirred on the stuffed owl. It was just an object. But the crocodile turned its attention from the others, and glared at Alex with hideous, evil interest.

Then its feet moved, scraping on the boards as it started to turn towards her.

"*Alex!*" shrieked Mags and Devi together. Mr Lawless and Imogen both tried to run towards Alex, but before they could take more than two steps the crocodile turned, with terrifying speed, and a hideous snarling roar rang through the hall as it blocked their path. Then its vicious little eyes fixed on Alex again. She was its prey. And this time, no one was going to stop it from getting her.

Alex knew she had to do something – but what? She looked around wildly – and inspiration struck a second time.

"Mr Lawless!" she yelled. "Catch!"

She snatched up the stag's head and threw it with all her strength towards him, and as the crocodile took a ponderous, sinister step towards her Alex threw the fox fur to Imogen. Then she grabbed the owl again.

"You've got to help us!" she shouted at it. "Come *on*! You've never tried to kill us, I know you don't want that! But this thing *will* kill us unless you do something to stop it!"

Realizing why she had thrown the props to them, Mr Lawless and Imogen started to shout at the stag and the fox.

"Come on!" roared Mr Lawless. "Wake up! *Wake up!*"

"Please!" cried Imogen, hugging the fox fur to her. And Alex begged, "If you don't help us, we won't be able to help you! Do this for us and we'll find you a home, I *promise*!"

The crocodile lumbered another step towards Alex. She heard its claws scraping on the boards. She saw its monstrous jaws opening, wider, wider. . .

Suddenly, from above her head came a furious screech, and a dark, feathered blur plummeted downwards at the crocodile. And suddenly they were there, all the animals, erupting from their hiding places behind the curtains, under the stage, out of the scenery. A clamour of noise rang through the hall – shrieking, squealing, snarling, hooting, baying – as every creature in the panto props launched itself at the rogue monster.

With an enraged bellow the crocodile whipped round. Its jaws snapped and lunged, but its attackers were too quick and agile for its clumsy fury. They pecked, they bit, they clawed, they kicked – and the form of the crocodile began to collapse. Alex and Mags were yelling without even realizing it, adding to the din as they spurred the animals on. The crocodile's shape was breaking up now, bits of it ripping away like fog in a wind.

And then—

And then, it was gone. Utterly vanished, as if it had never existed.

The noise died down until the hall was completely silent. The animals stood or sat still, their bright eyes regarding the five stunned humans. The owl – perched on a trestle table now – blinked, and flapped its wings once.

Then calmly and quietly the creatures all turned towards the scattered pile of props. They moved towards them, and, eerily, they seemed to melt into them. Alex felt the stuffed owl quiver as the real owl (but which owl *was* real? She didn't know any more) blended with it and vanished. From the corner of her eye she saw the snake-skin gloves wriggle and then lie motionless.

And then, only the props were left.

No one said a word for what seemed a very long time. Then, at last, Mags started to giggle.

It was half hysteria and half relief, and within seconds everyone else caught it and no one could make it stop. When it finally did, they all suddenly felt very serious and sober.

"We've got to help them," said Devi quietly.

"Alex promised, after all," added Mags. She smiled weakly at Alex. "If she hadn't. . ."

"Let's not think about that," said Mr Lawless. "Alex, just before the – well, before that last thing happened – you said, "'What if we. . .'"

"Yes." Alex walked slowly over to where the fox-fur wrap lay on the floor. She picked it up. Gently, affectionately, she stroked it. Then she smiled.

"You're all going to think I'm totally crazy. But this is what I thought we could do. . ."

Alex couldn't see the audience, but she could hear them laughing over the music, and a grin spread across her face. The panto was going better than anyone had dreamed. No one had messed up their lines, none of the scenery had fallen down, and even the teddy bears had got through their dance without crashing into each other.

There was loud applause when the music stopped, and Alex checked her script again as she got ready to do the next animal voice. Then the audience started to boo and hiss, and a *click-click* of stiletto heels announced Mags's entrance. Alex could just picture her leering and menacing with her fingernails, and twirling the fox fur to make the crowd hate her even more.

One thing was missing from Horrida's costume now, though. The handbag. Mr Lawless had consigned that bag to the school's central heating boiler, and no one was more thankful than Alex to know that it was gone forever.

As for the other creatures, though. . .

"*Mirror, mirror, on the wall,*

Who is the fairest of them all?"

Mags's voice rang out evilly, and Alex put her mouth to the little gap behind which the stuffed owl had been placed.

"*Not yoooou! So POOOOH!*" she hooted.

And from somewhere close by came an answering sound, so soft that only Alex could hear it. Not quite a hoot and not quite a chuckle, but with a little bit of both. The owl, it seemed, was enjoying the joke. Just like the fox and badger and stag and rabbits and mice. Oh, Alex had glimpsed their little furry faces peeking out from their new home, which they seemed so pleased with.

Because the animals were now living – if living was quite the word for it – in the painted scenery. It was the perfect place for them, just what they'd been used to when they were alive. After the panto was over, the Lawlesses were going to take the scenery home, and Imogen had said she would set it all up, with the props, in her studio, where there was plenty of room and it need never be disturbed. It would be fun, she'd added, to think that the animals were around, and she was sure they'd behave themselves and not get up to *too* much mischief.

So the animals had a new home at last. It wasn't a real wood, of course. But, as Mags had said, the animals weren't real either; not properly. But perhaps the scenery had a spirit; not in the cardboard and paint and papier-mâché, but in the *meaning* of it. And that was enough to make the animals' own spirits happy.

Mags was hamming up a fine old storm now as Horrida ranted and raved, and the audience were rolling in their seats. Time for the stag voice in a moment; Mr Lawless, as Baron Beastly, had just come in, and every time he said "Yes, dear" to Horrida, the stag made a honking noise. Caroly had thought that one up. Maybe she was improving. . .

Alex grinned again. Caroly was out there somewhere in the audience. Chaz too. Mr Lawless had had a long talk with both of them, and they were getting over their fear. Though they'd probably never, ever say another word about it to anyone else. After all, who'd believe them?

Another soft sound answered her thought, as if something had read her mind and was amused.

Which it probably was. *We all know the truth, don't we?* thought Alex. *And, as Mr Lawless would say, it's much, much stranger than fiction.*

Everyone agreed that the show had been a roaring success – the best, they said, that the school had put on in years. The party afterwards, for cast and teachers and parents, was a celebration on a grand scale. But now it was over. The last car had driven away. Weary but contented people were collapsing into their beds. And the school, under its covering of gently falling snow, stood silent and dark.

In the hall, the stage curtains were closed. The chairs and the scenery were still in place, because there were two more performances still to do. But there was no flutter or scuttle of movement among the painted flats. There was only a sense of peace; as though everything living – or once living – was soundly asleep.

Until, from beneath the stage, there came a sound. It was only a small sound. A slight scraping, then a scuffle. And then a slithering, slapping noise; as if something very large, and not at all pleasant, was moving carefully among the struts and boards.

Slowly, it emerged. If anyone had been there, they would have seen that it was smoky-grey and ghostlike, the outlines of the hall visible through its long, bulky shape.

But no one was there. No one at all.

Yet.

The phantom raised its huge head. Its jaws parted, showing a mouthful of teeth.

And, in the way that only a crocodile can, it *smiled*.

Are they ordinary animals – or are they

Creatures ...?

Don't miss

See How They Run

by Louise Cooper

Turn the page and read on

Creatures – you have been warned!

The ugly truth dawned on Jon even before he started to swing the torch around in a wide arc. There were rats everywhere. Dozens and dozens of them, perched on the rubble, squatting on the broken timbers, lurking in every cranny. Not a muscle twitched and not a whisker moved. But the cold gaze of each and every rat was fixed unwaveringly on his face.

Jon started to feel sick. He wasn't squeamish about rats; in the ordinary way he wasn't scared of them at all. This, though, was different. There was something horribly *knowing* about the way these rats were looking at him. It was almost as if they had one single mind.

Or as if something far, far more intelligent was controlling them. . .

He took an unsteady step backwards. As one, the rats on the floor moved as well, keeping precisely the same distance between themselves and him. Another step, another quick movement. And now the ones on the fallen beam were closing in. They didn't take their eyes off him for an instant. Suddenly, unpleasantly, Jon realized that by backing away from them, he was getting nearer to the hole in the floor.

Which was, perhaps, exactly what they wanted him to do.

Don't panic! Jon's floundering brain told him. The rats were trying to drive him towards the hole, but he didn't have to obey. However many of them there were, he was far bigger and stronger. All he had to do was step over them – jump over them, if necessary – and run for the door. They couldn't stop him. They *couldn't*.

He drew a huge breath, and lunged forward.

Everything happened so fast then that it was blurring chaos in Jon's mind. A shrill, racketing noise echoed through the room – it was the rats squealing, though he didn't know it then – and from behind him came a slither and a *whoosh*. An enormous shadow flicked across his wildly swinging torch beam, and something big and dark barrelled at him from behind.

Craig's Crocodile

by Jillian Powell

Illustrated by Peter Kavanagh

Now listen girls and boys –

there's a story to be told.

It's about a man called Ron

and a crocodile he sold.

They called Ron “Mr Pet” –
he sold pets of every size,

from rabbits with big ears,

to bushbabies with big eyes.

But the secret of a pet
is to get one right for you.

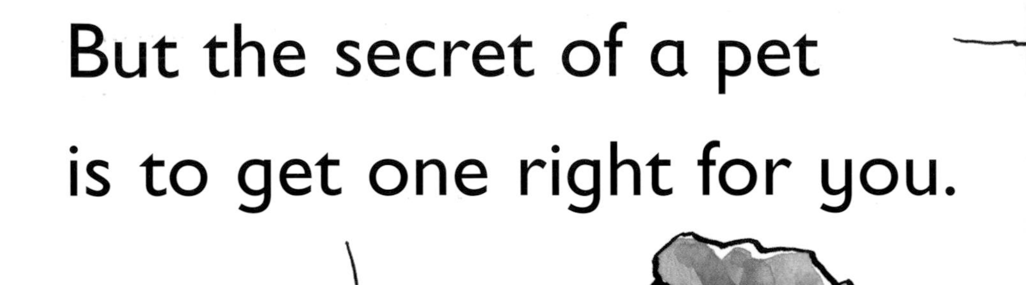

If your home is very small,

then your pet must
be small, too!

Now a crocodile
needs space,
for he likes to slide
and swim.

So to keep one in a bath
would be very cruel to him.

But along comes little Craig,
and he wants a pet
that's cool ...

... not a budgie like

at Gran's,

or a hamster like
at school.

When Craig sees
a baby croc,
he thinks it's
kind of cute.

So he pays the price to Ron,

and Dad puts it in the boot.

Mr Pet is feeling rich.
He doesn't care that
Craig's a child!

And he never thought
to warn them
that a crocodile is
WILD!

And it grows and
grows each day,
till it reaches its full size.

Which is bigger than a bath ...

... as Craig found to

his surprise!

Leapfrog has been specially designed to fit the requirements of the National Literacy Strategy. It offers real books for beginning readers by top authors and illustrators. There are 55 Leapfrog stories to choose from:

The Bossy Cockerel
ISBN 978 0 7496 3828 3

Bill's Baggy Trousers
ISBN 978 0 7496 3829 0

Little Joe's Big Race
ISBN 978 0 7496 3832 0

The Little Star
ISBN 978 0 7496 3833 7

The Cheeky Monkey
ISBN 978 0 7496 3830 6

Selfish Sophie
ISBN 978 0 7496 4385 0

Recycled!
ISBN 978 0 7496 4388 1

Felix on the Move
ISBN 978 0 7496 4387 4

Pippa and Poppa
ISBN 978 0 7496 4386 7

Jack's Party
ISBN 978 0 7496 4389 8

The Best Snowman
ISBN 978 0 7496 4390 4

Mary and the Fairy
ISBN 978 0 7496 4633 2

The Crying Princess
ISBN 978 0 7496 4632 5

Jasper and Jess
ISBN 978 0 7496 4081 1

The Lazy Scarecrow
ISBN 978 0 7496 4082 8

The Naughty Puppy
ISBN 978 0 7496 4383 6

FAIRY TALES

Cinderella
ISBN 978 0 7496 4228 0

The Three Little Pigs
ISBN 978 0 7496 4227 3

Jack and the Beanstalk
ISBN 978 0 7496 4229 7

The Three Billy Goats Gruff
ISBN 978 0 7496 4226 6

Goldilocks and the Three Bears
ISBN 978 0 7496 4225 9

Little Red Riding Hood
ISBN 978 0 7496 4224 2

Rapunzel
ISBN 978 0 7496 6159 5

Snow White
ISBN 978 0 7496 6161 8

The Emperor's New Clothes
ISBN 978 0 7496 6163 2

The Pied Piper of Hamelin
ISBN 978 0 7496 6164 9

Hansel and Gretel
ISBN 978 0 7496 6162 5

The Sleeping Beauty
ISBN 978 0 7496 6160 1

Rumpelstiltskin
ISBN 978 0 7496 6165 6

The Ugly Duckling
ISBN 978 0 7496 6166 3

Puss in Boots
ISBN 978 0 7496 6167 0

The Frog Prince
ISBN 978 0 7496 6168 7

The Princess and the Pea
ISBN 978 0 7496 6169 4

Dick Whittington
ISBN 978 0 7496 6170 0

The Elves and the Shoemaker
ISBN 978 0 7496 6581 4

The Little Match Girl
ISBN 978 0 7496 6582 1

The Little Mermaid
ISBN 978 0 7496 6583 8

The Little Red Hen
ISBN 978 0 7496 6585 2

The Nightingale
ISBN 978 0 7496 6586 9

Thumbelina
ISBN 978 0 7496 6587 6

RHYME TIME

Mr Spotty's Potty
ISBN 978 0 7496 3831 3

Eight Enormous Elephants
ISBN 978 0 7496 4634 9

Freddie's Fears
ISBN 978 0 7496 4382 9

Squeaky Clean
ISBN 978 0 7496 6805 1

Craig's Crocodile
ISBN 978 0 7496 6806 8

Felicity Floss: Tooth Fairy
ISBN 978 0 7496 6807 5

Captain Cool
ISBN 978 0 7496 6808 2

Monster Cake
ISBN 978 0 7496 6809 9

The Super Trolley Ride
ISBN 978 0 7496 6810 5

The Royal Jumble Sale
ISBN 978 0 7496 6811 2

But, Mum!
ISBN 978 0 7496 6812 9

Dan's Gran's Goat
ISBN 978 0 7496 6814 3

Lighthouse Mouse
ISBN 978 0 7496 6815 0

Big Bad Bart
ISBN 978 0 7496 6816 7

Ron's Race
ISBN 978 0 7496 6817 4